# THE BRIDGES AT TOKO-RI

# THE BRIDGES
# AT TOKO-RI

### A NOVEL

# JAMES A.
# MICHENER

**THE DIAL PRESS**

**NEW YORK**

*The Bridges at Toko-Ri* is a work of historical fiction. Apart from the well-known actual people, events, and locales that figure in the narrative, all names, characters, places, and incidents are the products of the author's imagination or are used fictitiously. Any resemblance to current events or locales, or to living persons, is entirely coincidental.

2015 Dial Press Trade Paperback Edition

Copyright © 1953 by James Michener
Introduction copyright © 2014 by Steve Berry

Published in the United States by The Dial Press, an imprint of Random House, a division of Penguin Random House LLC, New York.

THE DIAL PRESS and the HOUSE colophon are registered trademarks of Penguin Random House LLC.

Originally published in hardcover in the United States by Random House, an imprint and division of Penguin Random House LLC, in 1953.

ISBN 978-0-8129-8673-0
eBook ISBN 978-0-8041-5147-4

www.dialpress.com

*Book design by Carole Lowenstein*

*To* MARSHALL U. BEEBE
*Jet Pilot*

# INTRODUCTION
## Steve Berry

I grew up in the 1960s, a time when the extent of reading material for kids was, to say the least, limited. R. L. Stine, J. K. Rowling, Suzanne Collins, and so many others had yet to come along. In fact, what we now know as the young adult genre had yet to be invented. Back then, at least for me, it was Hardy Boys and Nancy Drew. A limited selection, but what gems those tales were—each loaded with action, adventure, secrets, and conspiracies. Wondrous stories to fuel young imaginations. I devoured them.

Then one day when I was sixteen years old, a friend handed me a dog-eared paperback copy of *Hawaii* by James Michener. Its thousand pages immediately intimidated me, as did the small print. I'd never seen so much information packed into one book. The opening sentence alone contained thirty-six words—monstrous in comparison to the prose of Franklin W. Dixon.

But what a sentence: *Millions upon millions of years ago, when the continents were already formed and the principal features of the earth had been decided, there existed, then as now, one aspect of the world that dwarfed all others.*

I kept reading.

What unfolded was a saga spanning many centuries that described how a tiny group of islands in the Pacific Ocean were formed by nature and then settled by man. The epic involved Polynesians, Chinese, Japanese, Europeans, and Americans. Its massive chapters, hundreds of pages long, featured one expansive episode after another—each intertwined—forming a chronicle that defined both the land and its culture. I read it cover to cover. Then I found more books by this guy Michener and read every one. Eventually, I started collecting them, and now, more than forty years later, I own a first edition of each, save one—*Tales of the South Pacific*. That book is hard to find. Only a few thousand were printed and, if by some miracle one of those 1947 first editions can be found, the price is through the roof. I keep every one of my Michener books prominently displayed, wrapped in plastic. I see them every day. They are a source of pride and comfort. Today, I write modern-day thrillers in which history plays a central role. Without question, the seed for that technique was planted the day I discovered *Hawaii*.

James Michener led an incredible life. Born in 1907, he was orphaned but was soon adopted by a woman named Mabel Michener, who was already raising two other children. Some of his biographers have hypothesized that he was actually Mabel's natural son, the adoption story used to protect both of their reputations. No one knows the truth, and as an adult Michener refused to comment on the subject.

By the time he turned ten, the family had moved to Bucks County, Pennsylvania. They were poor, barely able to put food on the table. His classmates, and even a teacher or two, tormented Michener about the secondhand clothes and toeless sneakers he wore every day. Later in life he recounted that taunting with a sly smile and a twinkle in his eye. He would say that those early years instilled in him an appreciation for life that he never forgot. They taught him about living simply and not attaching too much value to material things. And though he eventually earned hundreds of millions of dollars from writing, he always feared ending up poor.

Before he'd even reached twenty years of age, Michener had traveled across the country in boxcars, by thumbing rides, or simply by walking. He worked in carnival shows and other odd jobs, and he visited all but three states. Of that time, he wrote in his 1991 autobiography, *The World Is My Home*, "Those were years of wonder and enchantment. Some of the best years I would know. I kept meeting American citizens of all levels who took me into their cars, their confidence and often their homes." He would also say that those wandering years spurred inside him an insatiable curiosity about people, cultures, and faraway lands.

In 1925 he entered Swarthmore College, a prestigious Quaker institution, on a four-year scholarship, graduating with highest honors. He attended graduate school in Scotland, then returned home and taught at a school in Bucks County. He eventually ended up in New York City, editing textbooks at Macmillan Publishing.

World War II changed everything. At age forty Michener enlisted in the navy, where he discovered the enchanting South Pacific. He earned the rank of lieutenant commander and was made a naval historian, assigned to investigate cultural problems on the various islands. A near-fatal crash landing in French New Caledonia altered the course of his life. He wrote in his autobiography, "As the stars came out and I could see the low mountains I had escaped, I swore: 'I'm going to live the rest of my life as if I were a great man.' And despite the terrible braggadocio of those words, I understood precisely what I meant."

That brush with death also made him realize what every soldier was experiencing during the war, and that one day, when the danger had passed, people might want to recall those things. So each night he began writing down observations, recording comments, describing people and places. Fifty years later, in 1991, he said:

> Sitting there in the darkness, illuminated only by the flickering lamplight, I visualized the aviation scenes in which I had participated, the landing beaches I'd seen, the remote outposts, the exquisite islands with bending palms, and especially the valiant people I'd known: the French planters, the Australian coast watchers, the Navy nurses, the Tonkinese laborers, the ordinary sailors and soldiers who were doing the work, and the primitive natives to whose jungle fastnesses I had traveled.

All of that became *Tales of the South Pacific*.

The story of how that first manuscript made it to print is typical Michener—an unexpected combination of skill, determination, and luck. Using a pseudonym, he submitted the work to Macmillan, the publisher he'd worked for before enlisting. He omitted his name because he knew the company had a strict policy against publishing anything by an employee. Once the war was over he definitely intended to return to work there, but at the time of the submission he was technically a naval officer and not an employee.

So the company bought the book, which was published in 1947. One year later *Tales of the South Pacific* won the Pulitzer Prize for fiction.

Michener changed publishers in 1949, moving to Random House, where he stayed for the rest of his life. More books followed—*The Fires of Spring, Return to Paradise, The Bridges at Toko-Ri,* and *Sayonara.* Also in 1949 he moved to Honolulu and soon began work on his most ambitious project to date. Four years of research and three years of writing were needed to produce *Hawaii.* Its epic scope, length, and breadth proved to be the stamp of Michener's trademark style, one he would master over the next forty years. Legend has it that he finished *Hawaii* on March 18, 1959, the day Congress voted to accept the islands as the fiftieth state.

In 1962 Michener ran for Congress as a liberal Democrat but lost. Then, in 1968, he worked as secretary of the Pennsylvania Constitutional Convention. Outer space was a lifelong interest, and he served on NASA's advisory council, an experience that led to his novel *Space.*

Honors were something Michener shied away from, but in 1977 Gerald Ford bestowed upon him the Presidential Medal of Freedom, the nation's highest civilian award. Eventually, he wrote nearly fifty books, including five on Japanese art. His work has been translated into multiple languages, and there are more than 75 million copies of his books in print. These latest editions, being rereleased with new covers, will only add to that already staggering inventory.

A myth associated with Michener speaks of his cadre of researchers, used to gather the enormous amount of historical detail included in each of his epics. The reality was quite different. Most of the work was accomplished with the help of only three secretaries. He was a disciplined writer, establishing a routine early in his career and maintaining it his entire life. An early riser, he would go straight to work, where he wrote using a manual typewriter. He then had a light breakfast, maybe a meeting or two, and went back to work until around one P.M. Evenings were a time to be by himself. In the final year of his life, at age ninety, he still kept to his daily routine, except he spent three days a week at a renal treatment center, undergoing kidney dialysis.

The treatment proved painful in a multitude of ways, perhaps the most difficult being that it prevented him from straying far from home. The man who'd visited nearly every country could no longer travel. He told an interviewer at the time, "I sit in the TV room and see shows on the big ships I used to travel or areas that I used to wander, and a tear comes to my eye. It's not easy."

And that explains his death—he simply decided there would be no more dialysis. Instead, he welcomed the end.

Michener died on October 16, 1997.

I recall the day vividly. A segment on the evening news reported that he was gone. A sadness came over me, as if I'd lost a close friend—which, in a sense, I had.

In preparation for writing this introduction, I reviewed many articles written just after Michener passed. Most came from folks who'd had some personal contact with him through the years—an experience that had clearly stuck in their memory. All of them recounted what happened as if they had been in the presence of a king or head of state. It seemed a privilege to have spent just a little time with James Michener.

And that legacy lives on.

Though he was known to be fanatically frugal, he gave away more than $100 million. Recipients of his generosity included libraries, museums, and universities. He donated $30 million to the University of Texas for the establishment of a creative writing program. Several million more went to the creation of the James A. Michener Art Museum in Pennsylvania. One wing of that building was named for his third wife, Mari Sabusawa Michener, who died before him, in 1994.

He never really liked talking about himself, and he could frustrate interviewers. "Famous is a word I never use," he would say. "I'm well known. I've written thirty or forty books. I've done a great deal. I let it go at that." He was extremely generous with his autograph, so much so that he once noted, "The most valuable books are those that aren't signed."

Of my own collection, only one bears his signature.

To the frequently asked question, "Which book are you most proud of?" he would just smile and say, "The one I'm working on next."

By no means was he perfect. He could be a difficult man to know. He wasn't the type to start conversations with strangers, and he detested small talk. He had few close friends, and those who counted themselves in that number knew to tread lightly. He could be abrupt, even rude, and quite aloof. After his death we learned that he utilized collaborators on some of the big books, a fact he refused to acknowledge in life. He was married three times and at one point maintained a mistress. He was a multimillionaire, yet he would constantly fret about not having enough money to pay his bills. And though he was an orphan himself and a cofounder of an adoption agency, in the 1950s he gave up his claim to an adopted child when he divorced his second wife.

All of which shows that he was human.

But still, what a remarkable man.

Michener possessed an incomparable ability to simultaneously enthrall, entertain, and inform. Nobody else could write a two-hundred-word sentence with such grace and style. And he chose his subjects with great care: the South Pacific (*Tales of the South Pacific, Return to Paradise*), Judaism (*The Source*), South Africa (*The Covenant*), the West Indies (*Caribbean*), the American West (*Centennial*), the Chesapeake Bay (*Chesapeake*), *Texas, Alaska,* Spain (*Iberia*), *Mexico, Poland,* the Far East.

Like millions of other readers, I loved them all.

I never met James Michener. I would have loved to tell him how he sparked the imagination of a sixteen-year-old boy, which led first to a lifelong love of reading, then to a career as a writer. When, in 1990, I decided to write my first novel, it was Michener who influenced me most. By the end of that decade, though, changes had firmly begun to take hold. Today you won't encounter many two-hundred-word sentences or millennia-long sagas involving hundreds of characters. Instead, in the twenty-first century, story, prose, and purpose are expected to be tight. In the Internet age—with video games, twenty-four-hour news, streaming movies, you name it—there is just little time for thousand-page epics. Toward the end of his life Michener gave an interview in which he doubted he would have ever been published if he'd first started in that environment.

Thank goodness he came along when he did.

Now his stories can live forever.

# CONTENTS

# CONTENTS

**SEA**

T HE SEA WAS BITTER COLD. FROM THE VAST EMPTY PLAINS OF Siberia howling winds roared down to lash the mountains of Korea, where American soldiers lost on patrol froze into stiff and awkward forms. Then with furious intensity the arctic wind swept out to sea, freezing even the salt spray that leaped into the air from crests of falling waves.

Through these turbulent seas, not far from the trenches of Korea, plowed a considerable formation of American warships. A battleship and two cruisers, accompanied by fourteen destroyers to shield against Russian submarines, held steady course as their icy decks rose and fell and shivered in the gale. They were the ships of Task Force 77 and they had been sent to destroy the communist-held bridges at Toko-ri.

Toward the center of this powerful assembly rode two fast carriers, the cause of the task force and its mighty arm. Their massive decks pitched at crazy angles, which for the present made take-offs or landings impossible. Their planes stood useless, huddled together in the wind, lashed down by steel cables.

It was strange, and in some perverse way resolutely American, that these two carriers wallowing in the dusk bore names which memorialized not stirring victories but humiliating defeats, as if by thus publishing her indifference to catastrophe and her willingness to surmount it, the United States were defying her enemies. To the east, and farther out to sea, rode the *Hornet,* whose predecessor of that name had absorbed a multitude of Japanese bombs and torpedoes, going down off Guadalcanal, while the inboard carrier, the *Savo,* would forever remind the navy of its most shameful defeat in history, when four cruisers sank helpless at Savo Island, caught sleeping by the audacious Japanese.

Now, as night approached the freezing task force, the bull horn on the *Savo* rasped out, "Prepare to launch aircraft!" And it was obvious from the way her deck was arranged that the carrier already had some planes in the skies over Korea, and every man who watched the heaving sea wondered how those planes could possibly get back aboard.

The bull horn, ignoring such problems, roared, "Prepare to launch helicopter!" and although the deck pitched in abandon, rotors began to turn, slowly at first and then with lumbering speed.

Now the great carrier struck a sea trough and slid away, her deck lurching, but relentlessly the bull horn cried, "Move jets into position for launching," and the catapult crew, fighting for footing on the sliding deck, sprang swiftly into action, inching two heavy Banshees onto the catapults, taking painful care not to allow the jets to get rolling, lest they plunge overboard with some sudden shifting of the deck.

"Start jet engines," roared the insistent bull horn.

The doctor, who had to be on deck in case of crash, looked at the heaving sea and yelled to the crane operator, "They may launch these jets, but they'll never get 'em back aboard."

The craneman looked down from his giant machine, which could lift a burning plane and toss it into the sea, and shouted, "Maybe they're planning to spend the night at some air force field in Korea. Along with the ones that are already up."

But at this instant all ships of the task force swung in tight circles and headed away from the open sea, straight for the nearby cliffs of Korea, and when the turn was completed, the deck of the *Savo* mysteriously stabilized. The effects of wind and sea neutralized each other, and planes returning from the bombardment of Korea now had a safe place to land.

But before they could do so the bull horn cried eerily into the dusk, "Launch helicopter!" and the crazy bird, its two rotors spinning so slowly the blades could be seen, stumbled into the air, and the horn cried, "Launch jets!"

Then, as the great carrier rode serenely amid the storms, the catapult officer whirled one finger above his head and a tremendous, almost unbearable roar arose and twin blasts of heat leaped from each Banshee, burning the icy air more than a hundred feet aft. Now the officer whirled two fingers and the roar increased and white heat scorched the deck of the carrier and the twin engines whipped to a meaningless speed of 13,000 revolutions a minute and the Banshee pilot, forcing his head back against a cushion, saluted and the catapult officer's right hand whipped down and the catapult fired.

Nine tons of jet aircraft were swept down the deck at a speed of more than 135 miles an hour. Within less than 150 feet the immense Banshee was airborne, and by the time it reached the forward edge of the carrier, it was headed toward its mission. Four times the catapults fired and four times heavy jets leaped into the darkening sky and headed for the coastline of Korea.

As soon as they had left, the bull horn wailed, "Respot planes. On the double. We must recover the Korean jets immediately."

When this announcement was made thirty old-fashioned propeller planes were already lashed down on the after part of the flight deck in precisely that area needed for landing the jets which now appeared overhead. The prop planes had been stowed there to permit catapult take-offs, and now they must be moved forward. So on the wooden deck, swept by icy winds, hundreds of young men in varicolored uniforms sped to the task of clearing the landing space. Men in green stowed the catapult gear so that no remnant of the powerful machine was visible. Other men in yellow leaped upon the deck and began to indicate the course each plane must follow on its way to forward stowage. Dozens of tough young men in blue leaned their shoulders against the planes, swung them laboriously into position and pushed them slowly into the biting wind. In blazing red uniforms other men checked guns or fueled empty craft while plane captains in brown sat in cockpits and worked the brakes to prevent accident. Darting about through the milling, pushing, shouting deck hands three-wheeled jeeps of vivid yellow and lumbering tractors in somber gray hurried to their jobs, while over all towered the mighty arms of the enormous black and sinister crane. Behind it lurked two weird men in fantastic suits of ashen gray asbestos, their faces peering from huge glassine boxes, ready to save the pilot if a crashed plane should burn, while in back of them, clothed in snowy white, the doctor waited, for death was always close upon the carrier deck.

So in an age of flight, in the jet age of incredible speed, these men pushed and pulled and slipped upon the icy deck and ordered the heavy planes with their bare hands. Upon trailing edges burdened with ice they pushed, their faces open to the freezing wind, their eyes heavy with frozen salt and the knuckles of their hands covered long since with protecting scars. And as they moved, their bright colors formed the pattern of a dance and after they had swarmed upon the deck for some minutes the *Savo* was transformed and from the lowering shadows the jets prepared to land.

This intricate operation was guided by one man. From the admiral's country he had directed the task force to run toward the communist coast. The last four jets had been dispatched at his command. He had placed the ships so that the operations of one would not trespass the allotted space of the other, and it was his responsibility to see that his carriers faced the wind in such position that smoke trailed off to one side rather than directly aft and into the faces of incoming pilots. Now he stood upon his bridge and watched the mountains of Korea moving perilously close.

Admiral George Tarrant was a tall narrow man with a sharp face that was sour and withdrawing like those of his Maine ancestors. Battlewizened, he had fought the Japanese with his own carrier at Saipan, at Iwo Jima and at Okinawa, where his austere and lonely presence had brought almost as much terror to his own fliers as it had to the enemy.

He was known through the navy as George the Tyrant, and any aviator who wanted to fetch a big laugh would grab a saucer in his left hand, a coffee cup in his right, lean back in his chair and survey the audience sourly, snorting, "Rubbish." Then the mimic would stare piercingly at some one pilot, jab the coffee cup at him and growl, "You, son. What do you think?"

But men who served with Tarrant soon forgot his tyranny and remembered his fantastic skill in operating a task force. His men said flatly, "He can do it better than anyone else in the world." He knew the motion of the sea and could estimate whether a morning swell would rise to prevent recovery of afternoon planes or subside so that even jets could land freely. He was able to guess when new gales of bitter Siberian air would rush the line of snowstorms out to sea and when the snow would come creeping softly back and throw a blizzard about the task force as it slept at night. And he had a most curious ability to foresee what might trouble the tin-can sailors serving in the remote destroyers.

He fought upon the surface of the sea and in the sky. He sent his planes inland to support ground troops or far out to sea to spot Russian submarines. His was the most complex combat command of which one man's mind was capable and on him alone depended decisions of the gravest moment.

For example, the position he was now in, with mountains closing down upon him, was his responsibility. Early that morning his aerologist had warned, "Wind's coming up, sir. You might run out of ocean by late afternoon."

He studied the charts and growled, "We'll make it."

Now his navigator warned, "We can't hold this course more than sixteen minutes, sir." The young officer looked at the looming coastline as if to add, "After that we'll have to turn back and abandon the planes."

"We'll make it," Tarrant grumbled as his ships plowed resolutely on toward the crucial hundred fathom curve which he dare not penetrate for fear of shoals, mines and submarines. But he turned his back upon his problem, for he could do nothing about it now. Instead, he checked to be sure the *Savo*'s deck was ready and in doing so he saw something which reassured him. Far aft, standing upon a tiny platform that jutted out over the side of the carrier, stood a hulking giant, muffled in fur and holding two landing-signal paddles in his huge hands. It was Beer Barrel, and if any man could bring jets surely and swiftly home, it was Beer Barrel.

He was an enormous man, six feet three, more than 250 pounds, and his heavy suit, stitched with strips of fluorescent cloth to make his arms and legs easier to read, added to his bulk. He was a farmer from Texas who before the perilous days of 1943 had never seen the ocean, but he possessed a fabulous ability to sense the motion of the sea and what position the carrier deck would take. He could judge the speed of jets as they whirled down upon him, but most of all he could imagine himself in the cockpit of every incoming plane and he seemed to know what tired and jittery pilots would do next and he saved their lives. He was a fearfully bad naval officer and in some ways a disgrace to his uniform, but everyone felt better when he came aboard a carrier, for he could do one thing. He could land planes.

He could reach out with his great hands and bring them safely home the way falconers used to bring back birds they loved. In the Pentagon they knew he broke rules and smuggled beer aboard each ship he served upon. Carrier captains knew it, and even Admiral Tarrant, who was a terror on navy rules, looked the other way when Beer Barrel staggered back after each drunken liberty, lugging his two ridiculous golf bags. The huge Texan had never once played golf and the two clubs sticking out were dummies. Once a deck hand, fearful that drunken Beer Barrel might slide back down the gangplank, had grabbed one of the outsize golf bags to help, but the surprising weight of it had crumpled him to the deck. Beer Barrel, barely able to heft the bag himself, had got it onto his massive shoulder, whispering beerily to the boy, "Thanks, Junior, but this is man's work." And he had carried the bags full of beer into his quarters.

For he believed that if he had a can of cold beer in his belly it formed a kind of gyroscope which made him unusually sensitive to the sea and that when this beer sloshed about it harmonized with the elements and he became one with the sea and the sky and the heaving deck and the heart of the incoming pilot.

"Land jets!" moaned the bull horn.

"Let's hear the checks," Beer Barrel said to his spotters, staring aft to catch the first jet as it made its 180° turn for the cross leg and the sharp final turn into the landing run. Now the jet appeared and Beer Barrel thought, "They're always pretty comin' home at night."

"All down!" the first watcher cried as he checked the wheels, the flaps and the stout hook which now dangled lower than the wheels.

"All down," Beer Barrel echoed unemotionally.

"Clear deck!" the second watcher shouted as he checked the nylon barriers and the thirteen heavy steel wires riding a few inches off the deck, waiting to engage the hook.

"Clear deck," Beer Barrel grunted phlegmatically.

He extended his paddles out sideways from his shoulders, standing like an imperturbable rock, and willed the plane onto the deck. "Come on, Junior," he growled. "Keep your nose up so's your hook'll catch. Good boy!" Satisfied that all was well, he snapped his right paddle dramatically across his heart and dropped his left arm as if it had been severed clean away from his body. Instantly the jet pilot cut his flaming speed and slammed his Banshee onto the deck. With violent grasp the protruding hook engaged one of the slightly elevated wires and dragged the massive plane to a shuddering stop.

Beer Barrel, watching from his platform, called to the clerk who kept records on each plane, "1593. Junior done real good. Number three wire." Never did Beer Barrel feel so content, not even when guzzling lager, as when one of his boys caught number three wire. "Heaven," he explained once, "is where everybody gets number three wire. Hell is where they fly wrong and catch number thirteen and crash into the barrier and burn. And every one of you's goin' straight to hell if you don't follow me better."

From his own bridge, Admiral Tarrant watched the jets come home. In his life he had seen many fine and stirring things: his wife at the altar, Japanese battleships going down, ducks rising from Virginia marshes and his sons in uniform. But nothing he knew surpassed the sight of Beer Barrel bringing home the jets at dusk.

There always came that exquisite moment of human judgment when one man—a man standing alone on the remotest corner of the ship, lashed by foul wind and storm—had to decide that the jet roaring down upon him could make it. This solitary man had to judge the speed and height and the pitching of the deck and the wallowing of the sea and the oddities of this particular pilot and those additional imponderables that no man can explain. Then, at the last screaming second he had to make his decision and flash it to the pilot. He had only two choices. He could land the plane and risk the life of the pilot and the plane and the ship if he had judged wrong. Or he could wave-off and delay his decision until next time around. But he could defer his job to no one. It was his, and if he did judge wrong, carnage on the carrier deck could be fearful. That was why Admiral Tarrant never bothered about the bags of beer.

On they came, the slim and beautiful jets. As they roared up-wind the admiral could see their stacks flaming. When they made their far turn and roared downwind he could see the pilots as human beings, tensed up and ready for the landing that was never twice the same. Finally, when these mighty jets hit the deck they weighed well over seven tons and their speed exceeded 135 miles an hour, yet within 120 feet they were completely stopped and this miracle was accomplished in several ways. First, Tarrant kept his carriers headed into the wind, which on this day stormed in at nearly 40 miles an hour, which cut the plane's relative speed to about 95 miles. Then, too, the carrier was running away from the plane at 11 miles an hour, which further cut the plane's speed to 84, and it was this actual speed that the wires had to arrest. They did so with brutal strength, but should they miss, two slim nylon barriers waited to drag the plane onto the deck and chop its impetus, halting it so that it could not proceed forward to damage other planes. And finally, should a runaway jet miss both the wires and the barriers, it would plunge into a stout nylon barricade which would entwine itself about the wings and wheels and tear the jet apart as if it were a helpless insect.

But it was Beer Barrel's job to see that barriers and the barricade were not needed and he would shout curses at his pilots and cry, "Don't fly the deck, Junior. Don't fly the sea. Fly me." An air force colonel watching Beer Barrel land jets exclaimed, "Why, it isn't a landing at all! It's a controlled crash." And the big Texan replied in his beery voice, "Difference is that when I crash 'em they're safe in the arms of God."

Now he brought in three more, swiftly and surely, and Admiral Tarrant, watching the looming mountains of Korea as they moved in upon his ships, muttered, "Well, we'll make it again."

But as he said these words his squawk box sounded, and from deep within the *Savo* the combat intelligence director reported coolly, "1591 has been hit. Serious damage. May have to ditch."

"What's his position?"

"Thirty-five miles away."

"Who's with him?"

"His wingman, 1592."

"Direct him to come on in and attempt landing."

The squawk box clicked off and Admiral Tarrant looked straight ahead at the looming coast. Long ago he had learned never to panic, but he had trained himself to look at situations in their gloomiest aspects so as to be prepared for ill turns of luck. "If this jet limps in we may have to hold this course for ten or fifteen more minutes. Well, we probably can do it."

He studied the radar screen to estimate his probable position in fifteen minutes. "Too close," he muttered. Then into the squawk box which led to the air officer of the *Savo* he said, "Recovery operations must end in ten minutes. Get all planes aboard."

"The admiral knows there's one in trouble?"

"Yes. I've ordered him to try to land."

"Yes, sir."

The bull horn sounded. "All hands. We must stop operations within ten minutes. Get those barriers cleared faster. Bring the planes in faster."

The telephone talker at the landing platform told Beer Barrel, "We got to get 'em all aboard in ten minutes."

"What's a matter?" Beer Barrel growled. "Admiral running hisself out of ocean?"

"Looks like it," the talker said.

"You tell him to get the planes up here and I'll get 'em aboard."

So the nineteen dark ships of the task force sped on toward the coastline and suddenly the squawk box rasped, "Admiral, 1591 says he will have to ditch."

"Can he ditch near the destroyers?"

"Negative."

"Is his wingman still with him?"

"Affirmative."

"How much fuel?"

"Six hundred pounds."

"Have you a fix on their positions?"

"Affirmative."

"Dispatch helicopter and tell wingman to land immediately."

There was a long silence and the voice said, "Wingman 1592 requests permission stay with downed plane till copter arrives."

The admiral was now faced with a decision no man should have to make. If the wingman stayed on, he would surely run out of fuel and lose his own plane and probably his life as well. But to command him to leave a downed companion was inhuman and any pilot aboard the *Savo* would prefer to risk his own life and his plane rather than to leave a man adrift in the freezing sea before the helicopter had spotted him.

For in the seas of Korea a downed airman had twenty minutes to live. That was all. The water was so bitterly cold that within five minutes the hands were frozen and the face. In twelve minutes of immersion in these fearful waters the arms became unable to function and by the twentieth minute the pilot was frozen to death.

The decision could not be deferred, for the squawk box repeated, "Wingman 1592 requests permission to stay."

The admiral asked, "What is the absolute minimum of gas with which the wingman can make a straight-in landing?"

There was a moment's computation. "Assuming he finds the carrier promptly, about four hundred pounds."

"Tell him to stay with the downed man . . ."

The voice interrupted, "Admiral, 1591 has just ditched. Wingman says the plane sank immediately."

There was a moment's silence and the admiral asked, "Where's the helicopter?"

"About three more minutes away from the ditching."

"Advise the helicopter . . ."

"Admiral, the wingman reports downed pilot afloat."

"Tell the wingman to orbit until helicopter arrives. Then back for a straight-in landing."

The bull horn echoed in the gathering dusk and mournful sounds spread over the flight deck, speaking of disaster. "Get those last two jets down immediately. Then prepare for emergency straight-in landing. A plane has been lost at sea. Wingman coming in short of fuel."

For a moment the many-colored figures stopped their furious motions. The frozen hands stopped pushing jets and the yellow jeeps stayed where they were. No matter how often you heard the news it always stopped you. No matter how frozen your face was, the bull horn made you a little bit colder. And far out to sea, in a buffeted helicopter, two enlisted men were coldest of all.

At the controls was Mike Forney, a tough twenty-seven-year-old Irishman from Chicago. In a navy where enlisted men hadn't much chance of flying, Mike had made it. He had bullied his way through to flight school and his arrival aboard his first ship, the *Savo*, would be remembered as long as the ship stayed afloat. It was March 17 when he flew his copter onto the flight deck, wearing an opera hat painted green, a Baron von Richthofen scarf of kelly green, and a clay pipe jammed into his big teeth. He had his earphones wrapped around the back of his neck and when the captain of the *Savo* started to chew him out Forney said, "When I appear anywhere I want the regular pilots to know it, because if they listen to me, I'll save 'em." Now, as he sped toward the ditched pilot, he was wearing his green stovepipe and his World War I kelly green scarf, for he had found that when those astonishing symbols appeared at a scene of catastrophe everyone relaxed, and he had already saved three pilots.

But the man flying directly behind Mike Forney's hat wasn't relaxed. Nestor Gamidge, in charge of the actual rescue gear, was a sad-faced inconsequential young man from Kentucky, where his unmarried schoolteacher mother had named him Nestor after the wisest man in history, hoping that he would justify everything. But Nestor had not lived up to his name and was in fact rather stupid, yet, as the copter flew low over the bitter waves to find the ditched plane, he was bright enough to know that if anyone were to save the airman pitching about in the freezing water below it would be he. In this spot the admiral didn't count nor the wingman who was orbiting upstairs nor even Mike Forney. In a few minutes he would lean out of the helicopter and lower a steel hoisting sling for the pilot to climb into. But from cold experience he knew that the man below would probably be too frozen even to lift his arms, so he, Nestor Gamidge, who hated the sea and who was dragged into the navy by his draft board, would have to jump into the icy waves and try to shove the inert body of the pilot into the sling. And if he failed—if his own hands froze before he could accomplish this—the pilot must die. That's why they gave Nestor the job. He was dumb and he was undersized but he was strong.

"I see him," Nestor said.

Mike immediately called to the wingman: "1592. Go on home. This is Mike Forney and everything's under control."

"Mike!" the wingman called. "Save that guy."

"We always save 'em. Scram."

"That guy down there is Harry Brubaker. The one whose wife and kids are waiting for him in Yokosuka. But he don't know it. Save him!"

Mike said to Nestor, "You hear that? He's the one whose wife and kids came out to surprise him."

"He looks froze," Nestor said, lowering the sling.

Suddenly Mike's voice lost its brashness. "Nestor," he said quietly, "if you have to jump in . . . I'll stay here till the other copter gets you."

In dismay, Nestor watched the sling drift past the downed pilot and saw that the man was too frozen to catch hold. So he hauled the sling back up and said, "I'll have to go down."

Voluntarily, he fastened the sling about him and dropped into the icy waves.

"Am I glad to see you!" the pilot cried.

"He's OK," Nestor signaled.

"Lash him in," Mike signaled back.

"Is that Mike? With the green hat?"

"Yep."

"My hands won't . . ."

They tried four times to do so simple a thing as force the sling down over the pilot's head and arms but the enormous weight of watersoaked clothing made him an inert lump. There was a sickening moment when Nestor thought he might fail. Then, with desperate effort, he jammed his right foot into the pilot's back and shoved. The sling caught.

Nestor lashed it fast and signaled Mike to haul away. Slowly the pilot was pulled clear of the clutching sea and was borne aloft. Nestor, wallowing below, thought, "There goes another."

Then he was alone. On the bosom of the great sea he was alone and unless the second helicopter arrived immediately, he would die. Already, overpowering cold tore at the seams of his clothing and crept in to get him. He could feel it numb his powerful hands and attack his strong legs. It was the engulfing sea, the icy and deadly sea that he despised and he was deep into it and his arms were growing heavy.

Then, out of the gathering darkness, came the *Hornet*'s copter.

So Mike called the *Savo* and reported, "Two copters comin' home with two frozen mackerel."

"What was that?" the *Savo* asked gruffly.

"What I said," Mike replied, and the two whirly birds headed for home, each dangling below it the freezing body of a man too stiff to crawl inside.

Meanwhile Admiral Tarrant was faced with a new problem. The downed pilot had been rescued but the incoming wingman had fuel sufficient for only one pass, and if that pass were waved off the pilot would have to crash land into the sea and hope for a destroyer pickup, unless one of the copters could find him in the gathering dusk.

But far more important than the fate of one Banshee were the nineteen ships of the task force which were now closing the hundred fathom mark. For them to proceed farther would be to invite the most serious trouble. Therefore the admiral judged that he had at most two minutes more on course, after which he would be forced to run with the wind, and then no jet could land, for the combined speed of jet and wind would be more than 175 miles, which would tear out any landing hook and probably the barriers as well. But the same motive that had impelled the wingman to stay at the scene of the crash, the motive that forced Nestor Gamidge to plunge into the icy sea, was at work upon the admiral and he said, "We'll hold the wind a little longer. Move a little closer to shore."

Nevertheless, he directed the four destroyers on the forward edge of the screen to turn back toward the open sea, and he checked them on the radar as they moved off. For the life of one pilot he was willing to gamble his command that there were no mines and that Russia had no submarines lurking between him and the shore.

"1592 approaching," the squawk box rasped.

"Warn him to come straight in."

Outside the bull horn growled, "Prepare to land last jet, straight in."

Now it was the lead cruiser's turn to leave the formation but the *Savo* rode solemnly on, lingering to catch this last plane. On the landing platform Beer Barrel's watcher cried, "Hook down, wheels down. Can't see flaps."

The telephone talker shouted, "Pilot reports his flaps down."

"All down," Beer Barrel droned.

"Clear deck!"

"Clear deck."

Now even the carrier *Hornet* turned away from the hundred fathom line and steamed parallel to it while the jet bore in low across her path. Beer Barrel, on his wooden platform, watched it come straight and low and slowing down.

"Don't watch the sea, Junior," he chanted. "Watch me. Hit me in the kisser with your left wing tank and you'll be all right, Junior." His massive arms were outstretched with the paddles parallel to the deck and the jet screamed in, trying to adjust its altitude to the shifting carrier's.

"Don't fly the deck, Junior!" roared Beer Barrel and for one fearful instant it looked as if the onrushing jet had put itself too high. In that millionth of a second Beer Barrel thought he would have to wave the plane off but then his judgment cried that there was a chance the plane could make it. So Beer Barrel shouted, "Keep comin', Junior!" and at the last moment he whipped the right paddle across his heart and dropped the left.

The plane was indeed high and for one devastating moment seemed to be floating down the deck and into the parked jets. Then, when a crash seemed inevitable, it settled fast and caught number nine. The jet screamed ahead and finally stopped with its slim nose peering into the webs of the barrier.

"You fly real good, Junior," Beer Barrel said, tucking the paddles under his arm, but when the pilot climbed down his face was ashen and he shouted, "They rescue Brubaker?"

"They got him."

The pilot seemed to slump and his plane captain ran up and caught him by the arm and led him to the ladder, but as they reached for the first step they stumbled and pitched forward, so swift was the *Savo*'s groaning turn back out to sea.

As soon as the copters appeared with little Gamidge and the unconscious body of the pilot dangling through the icy air, Admiral Tarrant sent his personal aide down to sick bay to tell the helicopter men he would like to see them after the flight doctor had taken care of them. In a few minutes they arrived in flag plot, Forney in trim aviator's flight jacket and Gamidge in a fatigue suit some sizes too large.

The admiral poured them coffee and said, "Sit down." Forney grabbed the comfortable corner of the leather davenport on which the admiral slept when he did not wish to leave this darkened room of radar screens, repeating compasses and charts, but Gamidge fumbled about until the admiral indicated where he was to sit. Pointing at the squat Kentuckian with his coffee cup, the admiral said, "It must have been cold in the water."

"It was!" Forney assured him. "Bitter."

"I hope the doctor gave you something to warm you up."

"Nestor's too young to drink," Forney said, "but I had some."

"You weren't in the water."

"No, sir, but I had the canopy open."

"How's the pilot?"

"When me and Gamidge go out for them we bring them back in good shape."

"They tell me he wasn't able to climb into the sling."

"That pilot was a real man, sir. Couldn't move his hands or arms but he never whimpered."

"Because he fainted," Nestor explained.

The admiral invariably insisted upon interviewing all men who did outstanding work and now he pointed his cup at Gamidge again. "Son, do you know any way we could improve the rescue sling?"

The little Kentuckian thought a long time and then said slowly, "Nope. If their hands freeze somebody's got to go into the water to get them."

The admiral put his cup down and said brusquely, "Keep bringing them back. Navy's proud of men like you."

"Yes, sir!" Forney said. He always pronounced *sir* with an insinuating leer, as if he wished to put commissioned officers at ease.

Then he added, "There is one thing we could do to make the chopper better."

"What's that?"

"I got to operate that sling quicker. Because it seems like Nestor goes into the sea almost every time."

"You know what changes to make?"

"Yes, sir."

"Then make them."

The two enlisted men thanked the admiral and as they went down the ladder Tarrant heard Forney ask, "Nestor, why'd you stand there with your mouth shut, like a moron? Suppose he is a mean old bastard. No reason to be scared of him."

"By the way," the admiral called. "Who was the pilot?"

"Brubaker, sir," Forney cried, unabashed.

The name struck Tarrant with visible force. He backed into the darkened flag plot and steadied himself for a moment. "Brubaker!" he repeated quietly. "How strange that it should have been Brubaker!"

Shaken, he slumped onto the leather davenport and reached for some papers which had been delivered aboard ship by dispatch plane that afternoon. "Brubaker!" He scanned the papers and called sick bay.

"Doctor," he asked, "any chance I could talk with Brubaker?"

A crisp voice snapped back, "Admiral, you know the man's suffered exposure."

"I know that, but there's an urgent matter and I thought that when he found himself in good shape . . ." He left it at that.

Then he thought of Brubaker, a twenty-nine-year-old civilian who had been called back into service against his will. At the start of the cruise he had been something of a problem, griping ceaselessly about the raw deal the navy had given him, but gradually he had become one of the two or three finest pilots. He still griped, he still damned the navy, but he did his job. The admiral respected men like that.

But Brubaker had a special significance, for on recent cruises Admiral Tarrant had adopted the trick of selecting some young man of about the age and rank his older son would have attained had the Japs not shot him down while he was trying to launch a navy fighter plane on the morning of Pearl Harbor. Tarrant found satisfaction in watching the behavior of such pilots, for they added meaning to his otherwise lonely life. But in the case of Harry Brubaker the trick had come close to reality. The Banshee pilot had the quick temper of his sons, the abiding resentments, the courage.

Admiral Tarrant therefore desperately wanted to leave flag plot and go down into the ship and talk with Brubaker, but custom of the sea forbade this, for the captain of any ship must be supreme upon that ship, and even the flag admiral who chances to make his quarters aboard is a guest. So Admiral Tarrant was cooped up in flag plot, a tiny bedroom and a special bridge reserved for his use. That was his country and there he must stay.

There was a knock upon the door and the aide said, "Sir, it's Brubaker!"

The good-looking young man who stuck his head in was obviously a civilian. He wore two big bathrobes and heavy woolen socks but even if he had worn dress uniform he would have been a civilian. He was a little overweight, his hair was a bit too long and he wasn't scared enough of the admiral. Indelibly, he was a young lawyer from Denver, Colorado, and the quicker he got out of the navy and back into a courtroom, the happier he'd be.

"You can scram now," he told the medical corpsman who had brought him up to the admiral's country.

"Come in, Brubaker," the admiral said stiffly. "Cup of coffee?" As he reached for the cup Brubaker didn't exactly stand at attention but the admiral said quickly, "Sit down, son. How's the Banshee take the water?"

"All right, if you fly her in."

"You keep the tail down?"

"I tried to. But as you approach the water every inclination is to land nose first. Then from way back in the past I remembered an October night when our family was burning leaves and at the end my mother pitched a bucket of water on the bonfire. I can still recall the ugly smell. Came back to me tonight. I said, 'If I let water get into the engines I'll smell it again.' So I edged the plane lower and lower. Kept the engines up and the tail way down. When the nose finally hit I was nearly stopped. But I was right. There was that same ugly smell."

"How was the helicopter?"

"That kind in back deserves a medal."

"They handle the rescue OK?"

"This man Forney. When I looked up and saw that crazy hat I knew I had it knocked."

Admiral Tarrant took a deep gulp of coffee and studied Brubaker across the rim of his cup. He knew he oughtn't to discuss this next point with a junior officer but he had to talk with someone. "You say the green hat gave you a little extra fight?"

"You're scared. Then you see an opera hat coming at you out of nowhere. You relax."

"I would. Forney was in here a few minutes ago. Put me right at ease. Implied I was doing a fair job. You've got to respect a character like that. But the funny thing is . . ." He looked into his cup and said casually, "Captain of the ship's going to get rid of Forney. Says the hat's an outrage."

Brubaker knew the admiral was out of line so he didn't want to press for more details but he did say, "The pilots'd be unhappy."

The admiral, far back in his corner of the davenport, studied the bundled-up young man and jabbed his coffee cup at him. "Harry, you're one of the finest pilots we have. You go in low, you do the job."

Brubaker grinned. He had a generous mouth and even teeth. His grin was attractive. "From you, sir, I appreciate that."

"Then why don't you stay in the navy? Great future here for you."

The grin vanished. "You know what I think of the navy, sir."

"Still bitter?"

"Still. I was unattached. The organized units were drawing pay. They were left home. I was called. Sometimes I'm so bitter I could bitch up the works on purpose."

"Why don't you?" Tarrant asked evenly.

"You know why I don't, sir. The catapult fires. There's that terrific moment and you're out front. On your way to Korea. So you say, 'What the heck? I'm here. Might as well do the job.' "

"Exactly. The President once rebuked me publicly. I'd had that big fight with the battleship boys because they didn't think aviation was important. Then the brawl with the air force who thought it too important. I know I'll never get promoted again. But you're here and you do the job.'"

"It would be easier to take if people back home were helping. But in Denver nobody even knew there was a war except my wife. Nobody supports this war."

At the mention of Brubaker's wife the admiral unconsciously reached for the file of papers, but he stopped because what the young pilot said interested him. "Every war's the wrong one," he said. "Could anything have been stupider than choosing Guadalcanal for a battleground? And look at us today!" With his cup he indicated on the chart where the permanent snow line, heavy with blizzards and sleet, hung a few miles to the east, while to the west the mountains of Korea hemmed in the ships. "Imagine the United States navy tied down to a few square miles of ocean. The marines are worse. Dug into permanent trenches. And the poor air force is the most misused of all. Bombers flying close air support. Militarily this war is a tragedy."

"Then why don't we pull out?" Harry asked bluntly.

Admiral Tarrant put his cup and saucer down firmly. "That's rubbish, son, and you know it. All through history free men have had to fight the wrong war in the wrong place. But that's the one they're stuck with. That's why, one of these days, we'll knock out those bridges at Toko-ri."

Flag plot grew silent. The two men stared at each other. For in every war there is one target whose name stops conversation. You say that name and the men who must fly against the target sit mute and stare ahead. In Europe, during World War II it was Ploesti or Peenemunde. In the Pacific it was Truk or the Yawata steel works. Now, to the navy off Korea, it was the deadly concentration of mountains and narrow passes and festering gun emplacements that hemmed the vital bridges at Toko-ri. Here all communist supplies to the central and eastern front assembled. Here the communists were vulnerable.

Finally Brubaker asked, "Do we have to knock out those particular bridges?"

"Yes, we must. I believe without question that some morning a bunch of communist generals and commissars will be holding a meeting to discuss the future of the war. And a messenger will run in with news that the Americans have knocked out even the bridges at Toko-ri. And that little thing will convince the Reds that we'll never stop . . . never give in . . . never weaken in our purpose."

Again the two men studied each other and the admiral asked, "More coffee?" As Brubaker held his cup the old man said gruffly, "But I didn't call you here to discuss strategy. I'm supposed to chew you out." With the coffee pot he indicated the file of papers.

"They crying because I wrecked that wheel?"

"No. Because of your wife."

The astonishment on Brubaker's face was so real that Tarrant was convinced the young man was unaware his wife and two daughters were in Japan. Nevertheless he had a job to do so he asked, "You knew she was in Japan?"

"She made it!" A look of such triumph and love captured Brubaker's face that the admiral felt he ought to look away. Then quietly the young man said, "This is more than a guy dares hope for, sir."

"You better hope you don't get a court martial."

"I didn't tell her to come," Brubaker protested, but such a huge grin captured his face that he proved himself a liar.

Tarrant kept on being tough. "How'd she get here without your help?"

"Politics. Her father used to be senator from Wyoming."

Brubaker closed his eyes. He didn't care what happened. Nancy had made it. In the jet ready rooms he had known many pilots and their women troubles but he kept out of the bull sessions. He loved one girl. He had loved her with letters all through the last war in New Guinea and Okinawa. The day he got home he married her and she'd never given him any trouble. Now she was in Japan. Quietly he said to the admiral, "If she's broken a dozen rules to get here it's all right by me."

The old man didn't know what to say. "War's no place for women," he grunted.

Then Brubaker explained. "If my wife really is in Japan, I know why. She couldn't take America any longer. Watching people go on as if there were no war. We gave up our home, my job, the kids. Nobody else in Denver gave up anything."

This made the admiral angry. "Rubbish," he growled. "Burdens always fall on a few. You know that. Look at this ship. Every man aboard thinks he's a hero because he's in Korea. But only a few of you ever really bomb the bridges."

"But why my wife and me?"

"Nobody ever knows why he gets the dirty job. But any society is held together by the efforts . . . yes, and the sacrifices of only a few."

Brubaker couldn't accept this, Tarrant realized, and he was getting mad in the way that had characterized the admiral's sons. The old man had learned to respect this attitude, so he waited for the young pilot to speak but Brubaker happened to think of his wife waiting in Japan and his anger left. "Look," he said. "It's sleeting." The two men went to the dark window and looked down upon the silent carrier, her decks fast with ice, her planes locked down by sleet.

"It'll be all right by dawn," the old man said.

"You ever hear what the pilots say about you and the weather? 'At midnight he runs into storms but at take-off the deck's always clear, damn him.'"

The admiral laughed and said, "Three days you'll be in Japan. No more worry about take-offs for a while." He slapped the papers into a basket. "I'll tell Tokyo you had nothing to do with bringing your wife out here."

"Thank you, sir."

Quickly the admiral resumed his austere ways. Shaking Brubaker's hand he said stiffly, "Mighty glad you were rescued promptly. Why don't you see if the surgeon can spare a little extra nightcap."

As soon as Brubaker left, Tarrant thought, "His wife did right. If mine had come to Hawaii when our oldest son was killed, maybe things would have been different." But she had stayed home, as navy wives are expected to, and somewhere between the bombing of Pearl Harbor, where she lost one son, and the battle of Midway, where her second was killed trying to torpedo a Japanese carrier, her mind lost focus and she started to drink a lot and forget people's names until slowly, like petals of apple blossoms in spring, fragments of her gentle personality fell away and she would sit for hours staring at a wall.

Therefore it angered Tarrant when civilians like Brubaker suggested that he, a professional military man, could not understand war. Quite the contrary, he knew no civilian who understood war as thoroughly as he. Two sons and a home he had given to war. He had sacrificed the promotion of his career by insisting that America have the right weapons in case war came. And now in Korea, of the 272 pilots who had initially served with him in his task force, 31 had been killed by communist gunfire. Tonight he had come within two minutes of losing Brubaker, the best of the lot. No one need tell him what war was.

He was therefore doubly distressed when the people of the United States reacted like Brubaker: "Hold back the enemy but let someone else do it." He felt that his nation did not realize it was engaged in an unending war of many generations against resolute foes who were determined to pull it down. Some of the phases of this war would no doubt be fought without military battles. Whole decades might pass in some kind of peace but more likely the desultory battles would stagger on and from each community some young men would be summoned to do the fighting. They would be like Brubaker, unwilling to join up but tough adversaries when there was no alternative. And no matter where they might be sent to serve, Tarrant was positive that they would hate that spot the way he and Brubaker hated Korea. It would always be the wrong place.

As if to demonstrate afresh how ridiculous Korea was, the aerologist appeared with the midnight weather reports from Siberia and China. Since these nations were not officially at war, their weather stations were required to broadcast their customary summaries, just as American and Japanese stations broadcast theirs. But since Korean weather was determined by what had happened in Siberia and China two days before, the admiral always had the tip-off and the enemy gained nothing.

"All wars are stupid," the old man grunted as he filed the Siberian reports. "But we'd better learn to handle the stupidity." He recalled England and France, dragging through their Korean wars for more than two hundred years. They had avoided panicky general mobilization and millions of citizens must have spent their lives without worrying about war until something flared up like Crimea, South Africa or Khartoum.

"And their wars weren't even forced upon them," he growled. Secretly he was frightened. Could America stick it out when dangers multiplied? If Englishmen and Frenchmen, and before them Athenians and the men of Spain, had been willing to support their civilizations through centuries of difficulty when often those difficulties were self-generated, what would happen to the United States if her citizenry abandoned the honorable responsibilities forced upon her by the relentless press of history?

He went up on the bridge to check the rolling sea for the last time. "What would they have us abandon to the enemy?" he asked. "Korea? Then Japan and the Philippines? Sooner or later Hawaii?" He walked back and forth pondering this problem of where abandonment would end, and as the sleet howled upon him he could not fix that line: "Maybe California, Colorado. Perhaps we'd stabilize at the Mississippi." He could not say. Instead he held to one unwavering conviction: "A messenger will run in and tell the commissars, 'They even knocked out the bridges at Toko-ri.' And that's the day they'll quit." Then reason might come into the world.

Upon that hope he ended the long day. He had checked the wind and the weather and the rolling of the sea and the number of planes ready for the dawn strike and the location of those storms that always hovered near his ships. He had posted the night watches and he could do no more.

# LAND

I
T WAS THE GREATEST LIBERTY PORT IN THE WORLD. IT HAD
more variety than Marseilles, more beauty than Valparaiso. Its
prices were cheaper than New York's, its drinks better than Lis-
bon's. And there were far more pretty girls than in Tahiti.

It was Yokosuka, known through all the fleets of the world as
Yu-*koss*-ka, and almost every man who had been there once had a
girl waiting for him when he got back the second time. For in the
cities near the port were millions of pretty girls who loved American sailors and their hilarious ways and their big pay checks. It was
a great liberty port.

Now as the *Savo* moved cautiously in toward her dock hundreds
of these girls waited for their sailors and thousands were on hand
for sailors they had not yet seen. Grim-faced guards kept the invad-
ers away from the ship, but the girls did gather outside the gates,
and among them on this windy, wintry day was one especially hand-
some girl of twenty dressed in plaid skirt from Los Angeles, trim
coat from Sears Roebuck, and jaunty cap from San Francisco. She
wore her jet hair in braids and kept a laugh ready in the corners of
her wide, black eyes. Her complexion was of soft gold and seemed
to blush as some of the other girls caught a glimpse of the *Savo* and
pretended they had seen her sailor.

"There's green hat!" they cried in Japanese.

"You don't worry about green hat," she replied, pressing against
the fence.

A comic among the girls put her right hand high above her head
and swaggered as she had seen Mike Forney swagger on earlier
leaves, and excitement grew as the *Savo* approached her berth. But
this morning the girls would have to stand in the cold a long time,

for there was a sharp wind off the sea and the lumbering bulk of the carrier presented so much freeboard for the wind to blow against that tugs with limited maneuvering space could not hold her from crashing into the quay, and emergency measures were clearly necessary. Accordingly the bull horn wailed the bad news, "F4U and AD pilots prepare for windmill."

Every propeller pilot cringed with disgust but none showed such outrage as one of the jet men. Stocky, florid faced, with a cigar jutting from his teeth, this forty-year-old Annapolis man whipped his bullet head and underslung jaw toward the bridge to see what stupid fool had ordered another windmill. As "Cag," commander of the air group, he was in charge of all planes and felt sickened as he watched the propeller jobs wheel into position. He was about to storm off the flight deck and raise a real row when Brubaker, standing with him, caught his arm and said, "Take it easy, Cag. You don't have to pay for the burned out engines."

"It's murder," the Cag groaned as his valuable prop planes were lashed down to the edge of the deck which threatened to crash against the quay. Their noses were pointed into the wind and their unhappy pilots sat in the cockpits and waited.

"Start engines," yowled the bull horn. Sixteen valuable engines revolved and sixteen sets of propeller blades tried to pull the big carrier away from the quay, but the effort was not sufficient, and the *Savo* appeared certain to crash.

"Engines full speed," moaned the bull horn and the noise on deck became great as the props clawed into the air and magically held the great ship secure against the wind.

This caused no satisfaction among the propeller pilots, for since their planes were stationary on deck, with no wind rushing through to cool them, each engine was burning itself seriously, and one plane mechanic rushed up to the Cag with tears in his eyes cursing and crying, "They're wrecking the planes! Look!"

One of the low-slung F4U's had begun to throw smoke and the Cag ran over to study it. He chomped his cigar in anger and said grimly, "They're killing these planes."

"Somebody's got to stop this," the mechanic said.

"I'm going to," Cag replied quietly and started for the admiral's plot, but before he could get there Brubaker hauled him down and the two men watched the propeller planes gradually ease up and allow the *Savo* to inch into her berth as gently as a fragile egg being laid into a basket by an old farm wife.

"Cut engines," rasped the bull horn and the Cag said bitterly, "Burn those engines up now and next trip over Korea the pilot bails out. This lousy captain thinks he has a new toy to play with."

"Save it for the hotel," Brubaker said. "Take it up with the admiral there." So the Cag turned away and as he did so Brubaker looked down from the carrier deck onto the quay and there stood Nancy and the two girls, dressed in winter coats and huddling together to protect one another from the wind. A great lump came into his throat and for a moment he could not wave or call, so that Mike Forney, who was marching up and down, impatient to burst ashore, asked, "That your family, sir?"

"Yes."

"It's worth bein' saved for them, sir." The way Mike said *sir* made Brubaker look to see if the cocky Irishman were kidding him, but Forney was staring raptly at Nancy and the two girls. "Hey, Mrs. Brubaker!" he roared. "Here's your hero."

Jumping up and down on her toes Nancy called excitedly to her daughters, "There's Daddy!" And they all threw him kisses.

Mike, watching with approval, said, "Right beyond that fence, sir, I got the same kind of reception waiting for me."

"You married?" Brubaker asked in astonishment. Somehow he had never thought of Mike as a family man.

"Not yet, but I may be. This shore leave."

"Some girl who came out with the Occupation?"

"Japanese girl," Mike said, adjusting his green hat at a night-club angle, but a messenger from the ship's executive officer arrived to inform Forney that the uniform of the day called for something more traditional and the insulted Irishman went below.

Immediately Brubaker wished that Mike had stayed, for the pain of seeing his women on the quay below was too great. They had come too far, they loved him too much and they reminded him too soon of icy Korea's waters clutching at him, trying to drag him down. For the first time in his life he became desperately afraid and wanted to leave the *Savo* right then, for he saw leading from the deck of the carrier, right above the bodies of his wife and daughters, four bridges stretching far out to sea and they were the bridges of Toko-ri and he was breathlessly afraid of them.

"Nancy," he whispered. "You should have stayed home."

But as soon as the ship's lines were secured, he dashed down the gangplank to embrace his wife and as he did so his youngest daughter caught him by the leg and began to babble furiously and from the way he bent down and listened to the excited little girl—as if he actually wanted to know what she had to say—every married man on the deck of the *Savo* towering above knew that Brubaker really loved his kids.

What the child said was, "I made a long airplane ride and now I know what you do on the ship." But Brubaker remembered the icy water and thought, "Thank God you don't know. And thank God your mummy doesn't, either." Then he laughed and caught the little girl in his arms and kissed her a lot and she said, "I like to fly airplanes like you, Daddy."

For Mike Forney reunions were somewhat less complicated, at first. Attended by silent Nestor Gamidge he strode to the gates of Yokosuka Naval Base, threw the marine on guard a nifty salute and stepped outside to freedom. He was a cocky figure, his fists jammed into his pea coat jacket, his uniform a trifle too tight, and it took him only a moment to find the girls. He stopped dead, thrust his big paw onto Gamidge's chest and cried, "Look at her, Nestor! Best-dressed girl in Japan!" Then he gave a bellow, rushed forward and caught Kimiko in his arms and kissed her lovely little cap right off her head.

"Hey, Kimiko! Fleet's in!"

To his astonishment she pushed him away, sedately picked up her cap and said, "Not so fast, big boy. We got to talk." And she led him to a bar and started patiently to explain the radically new situation, the one which was to cause the two riots.

For the officers of the *Savo* the Tokyo brass had reserved rest and recuperation rooms at the Fuji-san, a meandering Japanese hotel whose exquisite one-storied rooms and gardens hung on a mountain top which commanded a superb view of Fujiyama. In the old days this had been Japan's leading hotel but for the first six years after the war it served Americans only. Now, in the transition period between occupation and sovereignty, it had become a symbol of the strange and satisfying relationship between Japan and America: the choice rooms were still reserved for Americans but Japanese were welcome to use the hotel as before; so its spacious gardens, bent with pine and cherry, held both Japanese families who were enjoying luxury after long years of austerity and American military men savoring the same luxury after long months in Korea.

No one enjoyed the Fuji-san more than Admiral Tarrant. He arrived on the second day of liberty, changed into civilian clothes, gathered about him his younger staff officers and forgot the rigors of Task Force 77. Other admirals, when they reached Japan, were whisked into Tokyo for press conferences where they sat on the edges of their chairs trying to say exactly the right and innocuous thing. They must not, for example, admit that they were fighting Russians, nor must they even indicate that any of our men were being killed. In this special war there were special rules to keep the people back in America from becoming worried.

Admiral Tarrant was not the man for such interviews. The navy tried it once and he had said bluntly, "We're fighting Russian guns, Russian radar, Russian planes and Russian submarines. And a hell of a lot of our men are being killed by this Russian equipment, manned by Russian experts." General Ridgway's headquarters in Tokyo had blown a gasket and the entire interview was made top secret and the navy was advised that whereas Tarrant might be terrific as a task force commander, "Send him to some good hotel when he gets ashore . . . and keep him there."

Now he lounged in the bar and watched a group of pilots pestering Beer Barrel. Ten minutes after the *Savo* docked, the landing-signal officer had grabbed for the bar stool and he had sat there for almost twenty-nine hours, lapping up the wonderful Japanese beer. "Look at him!" one Banshee pilot cried. "He's goin' crazy. Doesn't know whether to claim Texas has the biggest midgets in the world or the smallest."

Four jet men, themselves pretty well hung over, formed a solemn circle about Beer Barrel and began to chant the carrier pilot's version of the Twenty-third Psalm:

> The Beer Barrel is my shepherd
> I shall not crash.
> He maketh me to land on flat runways: he bringeth me in
>    off the rough waters.
> He restoreth my confidence.
> Yea, though I come stalling into the groove at sixty knots, I
>    shall fear no evil: for he is with me; his arm and his
>    paddle, they comfort me.
> He prepareth a deck before me in the presence of mine
>    enemies; he attacheth my hook to the wire; my deck
>    space runneth over.

Admiral Tarrant laughed at the nonsense. Since his big operation two years ago he drank only coffee, but he often growled, "Just because I'm a reformed drunk no reason why I should deny pleasure to others." He poured himself some inky black coffee and looked into the gardens, where he saw Harry Brubaker's wonderfully lovely wife and her two daughters and they reminded him of what wars were all about. "You don't fight to protect warships or old men. Like the book says, you fight to save your civilization. And so often it seems that civilization is composed mainly of the things women and children want."

Then the admiral grew glum, for Mrs. Brubaker had told him at lunch, "If the government dared to ask women like me, this stupid war would end tomorrow." There lay the confusion. These bright, lovely women, whose husbands had to do the fighting, wanted to end the war on any terms; but these same women, whose children would have to live through servitude or despair should America ever be occupied, would be the precise ones who would goad their men into revitalization and freedom. So Admiral Tarrant never argued with women because in their own deep way they were invariably right. No more war . . . but no humiliation. He hoped to see the day when this difficult program could be attained.

But a more present problem was at hand, for the Cag stormed

across the garden, his cigar jutting belligerently ahead like a mine sweeper. The tough airman was known throughout the navy as a fireball and this time Tarrant, himself an airman, knew the Cag was right. The *Savo*'s use of windmill had been intemperate, a perversion of aircraft engines, but a deeper concern was involved, so the admiral prepared to squelch the likeable hothead.

For the navy high command had secretly asked Tarrant to send in a concurrent report upon this demon flier when his Korean duty ended. It was hinted that a bright and brash young man was needed for rapid promotion to a command of real authority and Tarrant guessed that the Cag was being weighed as an eventual task force commander. "It's a big job," the admiral mused.

He could recall that day in 1945 when Admiral Halsey commanded a supreme force built of five components each twice as large as present Task Force 77. It was so vast it blackened the sea with more than twenty carriers. It stretched for miles and ultimately it sank the entire Japanese fleet. One brain had commanded that incredible force and it behooved the United States to have other men ready for the job, should such a task force ever again be needed.

Long ago Tarrant had begun to argue that some new weapon— rockets perhaps or pilotless planes of vast speed—would inevitably constitute the task force of the future. He had seen so much change, indeed had spurred it on, that he could not rely perpetually on ships or airplanes or any one device. But until America was secure behind the protection of some new agency that could move about the earth with security and apply pressure wherever the enemy chose to assault us, it would be wise to have young officers trained to command a sea burdened with ships and speckled with the shadows of a thousand planes.

Perhaps the Cag was such a man. A lot of navy people thought so but no one knew for sure whether he had those two ultimate requirements for vast command: had he a resolute spirit and had he due regard for human life?

The Cag jammed his cigar through the door and asked, "May I speak with you, sir?"

Tarrant liked the younger man's brusque approach. "Sit down. Whisky?"

"Please."

"What's wrong?"

The Cag sailed right in. Chomping his cigar he snorted, "These lazy carrier captains. They're burning up our engines."

Tarrant thought he'd better let the fireball have it right between the eyes. Staring coldly he asked, "You think you could handle a carrier better?"

This stunned the Cag and he fumbled for a moment. Then, fortunately, the bar boy arrived with his drink and he grabbed for it. "You not having one, sir?" he asked.

"You know the doctor made me lay off," the admiral explained coldly.

Such treatment threw the Cag off balance, for he knew Tarrant's power in the navy. The old man may have queered his own promotion but he was still known as the incorruptible and his judgment on the promotions of others was prized.

In the embarrassing silence Tarrant asked grimly, "What's your major complaint against the carrier captains?"

The veins stood out on the Cag's bullet head, but he stamped his cigar out and said firmly, "They shouldn't burn up our propeller planes."

"How would you berth a big ship against the wind?"

"In the old days I would have waited. But whatever I did I wouldn't run a lashed-down engine at top speed."

Admiral Tarrant stared impersonally at Fujiyama, the wonderful mountain, and although he wanted to agree with Cag, he pondered precisely what question would most completely throw this young hothead off balance. Finally he settled on: "So you'd have a group of complaining F4U pilots dictate naval procedure?"

Again the Cag was staggered. "Sir, I . . ." He fumbled for words and then blurted out with startling force, "Sir, an engine has only so many good hours. If you burn them up on deck . . ." He fumbled again and ended weakly, "Why can't they use half-power?"

The admiral turned slowly away from Fujiyama and asked bleakly, "Do you consider an F4U engine more valuable than a carrier?"

The Cag retreated. "What I was trying to say . . ."

"Another whisky?"

The Cag needed something to restore his confidence but reasoned that if the old man was in an evil mood he'd better not accept two drinks, so he said lamely, "Thank you, sir, but I have a reservation for one of the sulphur baths."

"They're fun," the admiral said mournfully and when the Cag awkwardly excused himself, the old man sagged into a real depression, for he found it ugly to watch a promising young commander back away from what he knew was right. "Well," Tarrant grumbled, "he's popular. He'll be able to wangle a desk job. But he's no good for command. And I'll have to say so when we get home." Grieved, he decided to leave the bar.

But before he could get away, young Brubaker and his pretty wife approached and it was apparent she had been crying. "She wants to talk to you," Brubaker said with the air of a young husband who hopes somebody else can say the magic word which he has been unable to find.

"My husband tells me you can explain why this war is necessary," she said. "I sure wish somebody would."

"It isn't necessary," Tarrant said. Then, seeing the Brubakers' surprise he added, "You two have something to drink?"

"May we join you?" Nancy asked.

"Doctor won't let me." Then, seeing the young people frown, he added humorously, "I have no vices, no ambitions, no family and no home."

"That's what I mean," Nancy said. "I can understand why you get excited about war. But we do have a home and family."

"I'm not excited about war," the admiral contradicted. "And I don't think it's necessary. That is, it wouldn't be in a sensible world. But for the present it is inevitable." He poured himself some coffee and waited.

"If it's inevitable, why should the burden fall on just a few of us?" Nancy pressed.

"I don't know. You take the other night when your husband . . ." Before he could tell of the ditching he saw Brubaker make an agonized sign indicating that Nancy knew nothing of the crash and the admiral thought, "Like the rest of America, she's being protected."

He salvaged the sentence by concluding, "Your husband bombed a bridge. Because he's one of the best pilots in the navy he knocked out two spans. He didn't have to do it. He could have veered away from the bridge and no one would ever have known. But some men don't veer away. They hammer on in, even though the weight of war has fallen unfairly on them. I always think of such men as the voluntary men."

Nancy fought back her tears and asked, "So until the last bridge is knocked out a few men have to do the fighting? The voluntary men."

"That's right. The world has always depended upon the voluntary men."

Before Nancy could reply, the bar boy hurried up and asked, "Is Lieutenant Brubaker here?" The boy led Harry to a back door of the hotel where Nestor Gamidge stood, bloody and scarred.

"I'm sure glad to see you, lieutenant," he gasped. His blues were ripped and his face was heavily bruised.

"What's up?"

"Mike's been in a terrible fight, sir."

"Where?"

"Tokyo. I came out in a cab."

"What happened?"

"He's in jail."

"A public riot?"

"Yep. His girl's marryin' a bo'sun from the *Essex*."

"You mean his . . . Japanese girl?"

"Yes, and if you don't come in he'll be locked up permanent."

Tokyo was sixty miles away and to rescue Forney in person would consume many hours of leave that he might otherwise spend with his family, so Brubaker said, "I'll phone the M.P.'s."

"Callin' won't help, sir. Mike clobbered two M.P.'s as well as the gang from the *Essex*."

"You two take on the whole town?"

"Yes, sir."

Brubaker had to grin at the vision of these two tough kids on the loose and made up his mind abruptly. "I'll help."

He hurried back to where Nancy and the admiral sat and said

quickly, "Admiral Tarrant, will you please see that Nancy gets dinner? There's been trouble in Tokyo and I . . ."

"Oh, no!" Nancy protested.

"Admiral, it's Mike Forney."

"Drunken brawl?"

"Girl threw him over."

Nancy pleaded, "On our second night, why do you have to get
mixed up with drunken sailors?"

Brubaker kissed his wife and said tenderly, "Darling, if Mike
were in China I'd have to help."

"But, Harry . . ." It was no use. Already he was running down
the long hallway.

When Nancy realized that her husband actually was on his way
to Tokyo, she looked beseechingly at Admiral Tarrant and pleaded,
"Who's this Mike Forney he thinks more of than his own children?"
Her eyes filled with tears and she fumbled for a handkerchief.

The admiral studied her closely and asked, "If you were freezing
to death in the sea and a man brought his helicopter right over your
head and rescued you, wouldn't you help that man if he got into
trouble?"

Nancy stopped crying and asked, "Did Harry crash at sea?"

"Yes."

She looked down at her white knuckles and unclasped her
hands. Very quietly she said, "You know your husband's at war.
You know he's brave. But somehow you can't believe that he'll fall
into the sea." Her voice trembled.

When she regained control Admiral Tarrant asked, "Has Harry
told you about the bridges? At Toko-ri?"

"No. He never talks about the war."

"You must ask him about those bridges."

Weakly she asked, "Is he involved with the bridges?"

"Yes. When we go back to sea, your husband must bomb those
bridges."

In a whisper she asked, "Why do you tell me this?"

He replied, "In 1942 I had a daughter as sweet as you. She was
my daughter-in-law, really. Then my son was killed at Midway trying to torpedo a Jap carrier. She never recovered. For a while she

tried to make love with every man in uniform. Thought he might die one day. Then she grew to loathe herself and attempted suicide. What she's doing now or where she is I don't know, but once she was my daughter."

Nancy Brubaker could hardly force herself to speak but in an ashen voice she asked, "You think that . . . well, if things went wrong at the bridges . . . I'd be like . . ."

"Perhaps. If we refuse to acknowledge what we're involved in, terrible consequences sometimes follow."

A strange man was telling her that war meant the death of people and that if she were not prepared, her courage might fall apart and instinctively she knew this to be true. "I understand what you mean," she said hoarsely.

"Let's get your little girls and we'll have dinner," Tarrant said.

But Nancy was too agitated to see her daughters just then. She pointed to the end of the bar where Beer Barrel lay at last sprawled upon his arms, his face pressed against the polished wood. "Will he fly against the bridges, too?" she asked.

When the admiral turned to survey the mammoth Texan his lean, Maine face broke into a relaxed smile. "That one?" he said reflectively. "He flies against his bridges every day."

When Brubaker and Gamidge reached Tokyo, night had already fallen and there was slush upon the wintry streets that lined the black moat of the emperor's palace. At the provost marshal's office a major asked sourly, "Why you interested in a troublemaker like Forney?"

"He's from my ship."

"Not any more."

"Major," Brubaker asked directly, "couldn't you please let me handle this?"

"A mad Irishman? Who wrecks a dance hall?"

"But this man has saved the lives of four pilots."

"Look, lieutenant! I got nineteen monsters in the bird cage. Every one of them was a hero in Korea. But in Tokyo they're monsters."

Patiently Brubaker said, "Mike's a helicopter pilot. The other night Mike and this sailor . . ."

The major got a good look at Nestor and shouted to a sergeant, "Is this the runt who slugged you?"

"Listen, major!" Harry pleaded. "The other night I ditched my plane at sea. These two men saved my life. This runt, as you called him, jumped into the ocean."

The major was completely unimpressed. Staring at Nestor he said scornfully, "I suppose the ocean tore his clothes. Did he get his face all chopped up jumping into a wave?"

"All right, there was a brawl."

"A brawl! A brawl is when maybe six guys throw punches. These two monsters took on all of Tokyo."

It was apparent to Brubaker that pleading along normal lines would get nowhere, so he asked bluntly, "You married, major?"

"Yep."

"Tonight's the second night in eight months that I've seen my wife and kids. I left them at Fuji-san to get Mike out of jail. That's what I think of these two men."

The major stared at the docket listing Mike's behavior. "You willin' to cough up $80 for the damage he did?"

"I'd pay $800."

"He's yours, but you ain't gettin' no prize."

A guard produced Mike Forney, his face a nauseating blue in contrast to the green scarf. "She's marryin' an ape from the *Essex*," he said pitifully.

"I suppose you tried to stop her."

"I would of stopped the ape, but he had helpers."

When they reached the narrow streets where hundreds of Japanese civilians hurried past, Mike begged, "Talk with her, please, lieutenant. She might listen to you."

He led Brubaker to one of the weirdest dance halls in the world. A war profiteer had cornered a bunch of steel girders and had built a Chinese junk in the middle of Tokyo. He called it the Pirates' Den and installed an open elevator which endlessly traveled from the first floor to the fifth bearing an eleven-piece jazz band whose blazing noise supplied five different dance floors. The strangest adornment of the place was a mock airplane, piloted by an almost nude girl who flew from floor to floor delivering cold beer.

The steel ship was so ugly, so noisy and so crammed with chattering girls that Brubaker wondered how anyone had known a riot was under way and then he met Kimiko, Mike's one-time love. She was the first Japanese girl he had ever spoken to and he was unprepared for her dazzling beauty. Her teeth were remarkably white and her smile was warm. He understood at once why Mike wanted her, and when she rose to extend her hand and he saw her slim perfect figure in a princess evening dress which Mike had ordered from New York, he concluded that she warranted a riot.

"I very sorry, lieutenant," she explained softly, "but while Mike at sea I lose my heart to *Essex* man. *Essex* not at sea."

"But Mike's a fine man," Brubaker argued. "No girl could do better than Mike."

Kimiko smiled in a way to make Brubaker dizzy and plaintively insisted, "I know Mike good man. But I lose my heart."

Things started to go black for Mike again and he shouted, "Not in my dress, you don't lose it!" And he clawed at the dress which represented more than two months' pay.

Kimiko began to scream and the owner of the Pirates' Den blew a shrill whistle and prudent Nestor Gamidge said, "We better start runnin' now."

"Not without this dress!" Mike bellowed.

Nestor handled that by clouting Mike a withering blow to the chin, under which the tough Irishman crumpled. Then Nestor grabbed him by the arms and grunted, "Lieutenant, sir. Ask the girls to push."

In this way they worked Mike out a back door before the M.P.'s could get to him, but in the alley Nestor saw that Mike still clutched part of Kimiko's dress. He pried this loose from the stiff hand and returned it to Kimiko, saying, "You can sew it back on." Upon returning to Brubaker he reported, "Japanese girls are sure pretty." But when Mike woke up, sitting in one of the gutters west of the Ginza, he said mournfully, "Without Kimiko I want to die."

Gently they took him to the enlisted men's quarters, where Gamidge put the rocky Irishman to bed. When this was done, the little Kentuckian laboriously scratched a note and tucked it into the lieutenant's fist: "We owe you $80. Mike and Nestor." Then Brubaker started the long trip back to Fuji-san, where his wife waited.

It was nearly three in the morning when he reached the Fuji-san, but Nancy was awake and when he climbed into bed she clutched him to her and whispered, "I'm ashamed of the way I behaved. Admiral Tarrant told me about Mike Forney."

"I wish he hadn't. But don't worry. Nobody ever crashes twice."

There was a long silence and she kissed him as if to use up all the kisses of a lifetime. Then she controlled her voice to make it sound casual and asked, "What are the bridges at Toko-ri?" She felt him grow tense.

"Where'd you hear about them?"

"The admiral." There was no comment from the darkness so she added, "He had good reason, Harry. His daughter-in-law had no conception of war and went to shreds. He said if I had the courage to come all the way out here I ought to have the courage to know. Harry, what are the bridges?"

And suddenly, in the dark room, he wanted to share with his wife his exact feelings about the bridges. "I haven't really seen them," he whispered in hurried syllables. "But I've studied pictures. There are four bridges, two for railroads, two for trucks, and they're vital. Big hills protect them and lots of guns. Every hill has lots of Russian guns."

"Are Russians fighting in Korea?"

"Yes. They do all the radar work. We have only two approaches to the bridges. The valley has one opening to the east, another to the west. When we bomb the bridges we must dive in one end and climb out the other." He hesitated and added quickly, "At Toko-ri there is more flak than anywhere in Germany last time. Because the communists know where you have to come in from. And where you have to go out. So they sit and wait for you."

They whispered until dawn, a man and wife in a strange land talking of a war so terrible that for them it equaled any in history. Not the wars of Caesar nor the invasions of Napoleon nor the river bank at Vicksburg nor the sands of Iwo were worse than the Korean war if your husband had to bomb the bridges, and toward morning Nancy could control her courage no longer and began to cry. In her despondency she whispered, "What eats my heart away is that back home there is no war. Harry, do you remember where we were when we decided to get married?"

"Sure I remember. Cheyenne."

"Well, when I was explaining to the girls about the birds and the bees Jackie looked up at me with that quizzical grin of hers and asked, 'Where did all this stuff start?' and I said, 'All right, smarty, I'll take you up and show you.' And I took them to the Frontier Days where you proposed and I almost screamed with agony because everything was exactly the way it was in 1946. Nobody gave a damn about Korea. In all America nobody gives a damn."

When the morning sun was bright and the girls had risen, Harry Brubaker and his wife still had no explanation of why they had been chosen to bear the burden of the war. Heartsick, they led their daughters down to one of the hotel's private sulphur baths, where they locked the door, undressed and plunged into the bubbling pool. The girls loved it and splashed nakedly back and forth, teasing shy Nancy because she wouldn't take off all her clothes, so she slipped out of her underthings and joined them.

They were cavorting in this manner when the locked door opened and a Japanese man entered. He bowed low to both Nancy and Harry, smiled at the girls and started to undress. "Hey!" Harry cried. "We reserved this!" But the man understood little English and bowed to accept Harry's greeting. When he was quite undressed he opened the door and admitted his wife and two teen-age daughters, who laid aside their kimonos. Soon the Japanese family stood naked by the pool and dipped their toes in. Harry, blushing madly, tried to protest again but the man said with painstaking care, "Number one! Good morning!" and each of his pretty daughters smiled and said musically, "Good morning, sir!"

"*Ohio gozaimasu!*" shouted the Brubaker girls, using a phrase they had acquired from their nurse. This pleased the Japanese family and everyone laughed gaily and then the man bowed again. Ceremoniously, father first, the family entered the pool.

By now Harry and Nancy were more or less numb with astonishment, but the pleasant warmth of the room, the quiet beauty of the surroundings and the charm of the Japanese family were too persuasive to resist. Harry, trying not to stare at the pretty girls, smiled at the Japanese man, who swam leisurely over, pointed to one of the Brubaker girls and asked, "Belong you?"

Harry nodded, whereupon the man called his own daughters who came over to be introduced. "Teiko, Takako," the man said. They smiled and held out their hands and somehow the bitterness of the long night's talking died away. The two families intermingled and the soft waters of the bath united them. In 1944 Harry had hated the Japanese and had fought valiantly against them, destroying their ships and bombing their troops, but the years had passed, the hatreds had dissolved and on this wintry morning he caught some sense in the twisted and conflicting things men are required to do.

Then he sort of cracked his neck, for he saw Nancy. His shy wife had paddled to the other side of the pool and was talking with the Japanese man. "We better hurry or we'll miss breakfast," Harry said, and for the rest of his stay they became like the spectators at the Cheyenne Frontier Days and they enjoyed themselves and never spoke of Korea.

Then shore leave ended in one of those improbable incidents which made everyone proud he served aboard a good ship like the *Savo*. Admiral Tarrant went aboard at noon and toward four Beer Barrel staggered up the gangplank with his two golf bags. Brubaker had obtained permission for Nancy to see his quarters but when she found how astonishingly small the room was and how her husband slept with his face jammed under two steam pipes she said she felt penned in and would rather stay on deck.

In the meantime hundreds of sailors and their Japanese girls had crowded into Yokosuka and in the lead were Mike Forney and Nestor Gamidge, accompanied by seven girls from the dance halls of Tokyo, Yokohama and Yokosuka. "I never knew there were so many girls," Nestor said to one of the plane captains. "Best thing ever happened to Mike was losing Kimiko to that ape from the *Essex*."

Mike agreed. When he had kissed his girls goodbye he swung onto the quay, elbows out, and pointed to the *Savo*: "Greatest flat-top in the fleet." Then he stopped dead for he saw that the *Essex* was alongside and there stood beautiful Kimiko, wearing the expensive plaid he had bought her. She was kissing her ape from the *Essex* and things went black. Clenching his fists, Mike lunged toward the lovers but little Nestor grabbed him.

Mike stopped, slapped himself on the head and muttered, "Sure, what's one girl?" With grandiloquent charm he approached Kimiko, kissed her hand and said loudly, "The flower of Japan." Then he grabbed the *Essex* man warmly and proclaimed, "The flower of the fleet. The best man won. Bless you, my children."

Then everything fell apart. For some loud mouth in the *Essex* yelled derisively, "And we could lick you bums in everything else, too."

Mike whirled about, saw no one, then looked back at golden Kimiko and she was beautiful in that special way and she was his girl. Blood surged into his throat and he lunged at the *Essex* man standing with her and slugged him furiously, shouting, "You lousy ape!"

Six *Essex* men leaped to defend their shipmate and stumpy Nestor Gamidge rallied *Savo* men and soon M.P. whistles were screeching like sparrows in spring and there was a growing melee with men in blue dropping all over the place. Mike, seeing himself about to be deluged by *Essex* reinforcements, grabbed a chunk of wood and let the ape have it across the ear, laying him flat. At this Kimiko started to scream in Japanese and Mike grabbed her hat and tried to pull off the pretty plaid jacket, bellowing, "Go ahead and marry him. But not in my clothes." Three *Essex* men, gallant to the end, knocked him silly.

The captain of the *Savo* witnessed this disgraceful riot and determined on the spot to get rid of Mike Forney, but Admiral Tarrant, surveying the brawl from flag bridge, thought, "I'd hate to see the day when men were afraid to mix it up for pretty girls." He called for his glasses and studied Kimiko, who knelt over her *Essex* man and all the sailors aboard the *Savo* and the officers too were a little more proud of their ship.

# SKY

**T**HE SUN HAD TO BE WELL UP OR THE PHOTOGRAPHS WOULDN'T be any good, so it was nearly 0945 when Harry Brubaker's jet catapulted violently across the prow of the *Savo* and far into the sky toward Korea. Ahead of him streaked a single Banshee with an extraordinary nose containing nine broad windows through which heavy cameras would record the bridges of Toko-ri.

While the *Savo* was in Yokosuka, other carriers were supposed to photograph the target but they had failed. When Cag bent his bullet head over their muddy films he growled, "What's the matter? They afraid to go down low? We'll show 'em how to take pictures," and he assigned himself the dangerous mission, choosing Brubaker to fly protective cover.

Now, as the two Banshees streaked toward higher altitudes Brubaker concerned himself with trivial details: "Lay off those even altitudes. Use 25,300. Makes it just that much tougher for the anti-aircraft crews. And remember that when Cag goes down for the pictures, keep 3,000 feet above him."

Then, in the perpetually mysterious way, when he had climbed into the higher atmosphere, he experienced the singing beauty of a jet as it sped almost silently through the vast upper reaches of the world. Sea and sky fell away and he was aloft in the soaring realm of the human spirit.

It was terrible and supreme to be there, whistling into the morning brilliance, streaking ahead so fast that the overwhelming scream of his engines never quite caught up. In this moment of exhilaration he peered into the limitless reaches of the upper void and felt the surging sensation that overtakes every jet pilot: "I'm out front." Through the silent beauty of this cold February morning he soared through the blue-black upper sky and thought, "I'm out front."

Then, as his eyes swept the empty sky in casual patterns, he uttered a stunned cry, "My God! There it is!" But when he looked directly at what he had seen it vanished, so he returned to scanning and from the powerful corner of his eye he saw it again, tremendous and miraculously lovely, one of the supreme sights of creation: Fujiyama in morning sunlight towering above the islands of Japan. The cone was perfect, crowned in dazzling white, and the sides fell away like the soft ending of a sigh, and somewhere on the nether slope Nancy and the girls were waiting.

He now looked at the majestic volcano with his full eye, but again it was the omniscient corner which startled him, for it detected the mountains of Korea. Dead ahead they lay, bold and blunt and ugly. Tortured and convoluted, they twisted up at the two fleeting jets, the terrible mountains of Korea. They were the mountains of pain, the hills of death. They were the scars of the world's violent birth, the aftermath of upheavals and multitudes of storms. There was no sense to them and they ran in crazy directions. Their crests formed no significant pattern, their valleys led nowhere, and running through them there were no discernible watersheds or spacious plains. Hidden among them, somewhere to the west, cowered the bridges of Toko-ri, gun-rimmed and waiting.

Brubaker knew the guns would be waiting, for as the Banshees crossed the coastline, a signal battery in Wonsan fired and he could follow the course of other gun bursts across Korea, for the communists announced impending danger exactly as the Cheyennes of Colorado had done two hundred years before.

Now the day's hard work began. As soon as the Banshees came in range of communist guns, Cag began to descend in swift jinking dips and dives to confuse ground gunners, never staying on either course or altitude for longer than fifteen seconds. This threw a special responsibility on Brubaker who stayed aloft, weaving back and forth lest some stray MIG try to pounce upon the preoccupied photographic plane. So imperceptible was Cag's silvery slim Banshee as it skimmed across the mountain tops that Brubaker was taxed to keep his eye on it.

At Yangdok a flurry of ground fire exploded at almost the right altitude to catch the photographic plane, so the jets increased speed to 560, jinking violently. Below them they spotted the ruins of a less important bridge, four spans rusting in the river. Farther on a communist working party strove to rebuild a major bridge, but this morning Cag ignored them, certain that later flights would halt the work. For now on the horizon rose the peaks that guarded Toko-ri.

Each was pock-marked with many circular red depressions in the snow. These were the gun emplacements and in swift estimate Brubaker decided there must be more than sixty. Lower were gaunt walled nests for the huge five-inch guns, a single shell from which could pulverize a plane before it fell to earth. And deep within the hills, hiding along the river, were the four bridges. On this first fleeting glance he noticed that the two historic bridges were on tall stone pillars and decidedly vulnerable, but that the two emergency alternates were extraordinarily low, scarcely clearing the water.

But most significant of all was one solemn fact: to get to the bridges you really did have to fly in one end of a valley, traverse it and fly out the other end. Brubaker swallowed and thought, "They got you lined up going and coming. And when you pull out for rendezvous you're a dead duck." Then he laughed to relieve his tension and whispered, "No wonder they saved this one till last."

At that instant Cag started his bold run into the western entrance to the valley. Pushing his nose down into a 40° dive, he screamed along the shimmering river, held courageously to the hairline railroad tracks, and roared upon the bridges at 580 miles an hour. During each inch of this run more than two hundred communist guns fired at the streaking Banshee, but it howled straight on, its cameras grinding, making no concession to the fire. Cag had one mission only, to bring back photographs, and he ignored everything else. Five-inch guns, three-inchers, machine guns and even carbines blazed at his wailing jet, but at last he pulled away from the mortal pit and with a sickening upward twist sped off to the north.

For a moment Brubaker lost the sleek Banshee as it fled to the hills for rendezvous. In some anxiety he cast his eyes swiftly left and right and thus caught a fleeting glimpse of the plane in the corner of his eye. Quickly rotating his vision in that area he gradually pinpointed the photographic plane, twisting and turning toward the safer hills. He had the sensation of spying upon an animal retreating to some sheltered valley after a wounding fight.

"Drop down and look me over," Cag called. "My tail section OK?"

Brubaker passed under the long-nosed jet and studied the fuselage minutely, for although both planes were doing more than 400 miles, in relation to each other they were nearly motionless. "Nothing visible," he reported.

"Back we go," Cag said.

The photographic jet heeled over in a tight turn, jinked to a lower altitude and went into a paralyzing dive. Out of the sun it streaked with blazing speed, but the communist gunners were waiting and in monomaniac fury they poured their fire upon the wraithlike Banshee as it screamed upon them. It seemed positively impossible that Cag could writhe his way through such fire but he bore on, clicking his shutters at the doomed bridges.

From aloft Brubaker followed this incredible mission and experienced a resolute desire to be there with his commander, but the instant this thought came to mind it was dispelled by the vision he had seen at Yokosuka: four bridges reaching out into space far above the heads of his wife and daughters, and he grew afraid; for he knew that tomorrow as the sun came up he would be pushing his own overloaded Banshee down, down upon the real bridges. It was then that the great fear came upon him, the one he would not be able to dispel.

Then he heard Cag cry, "Well, home we go."

Ecstatically the two jets zoomed to 26,000. Far below them the savage, cheated mountains of Korea began to assume a beautiful countenance. Gone were the tortured profiles and the senseless confusion, for with the bridges of Toko-ri behind him, Brubaker saw Korea with a kindlier eye. To the north sprawling reservoirs glistened like great brooches, holding the hills together. To the south snow hung upon the ridge lines and made the valleys shimmering wonderlands of beauty, while beyond the upcoming range of mountains lay the vast blue sea, bearing somewhere upon its bosom the task force, that fair circle of home, with Beer Barrel waiting on the after deck.

Even Cag was impressed and called, "Real estate sure looks better on the way home."

But when they reached home there was dismal news. "You heard the hot scoop?" Harry's plane captain asked as soon as Brubaker was out of the cockpit.

"We ordered home?"

"Forney and Gamidge are being sent to the barge."

"The barge?" This was a scow stationed near the Korean coast, and helicopter men with that duty lived miserably and engaged in one dangerous land mission after another.

A destroyer moved in and the last the *Savo* saw of Mike Forney was when he climbed into the bo'sun's chair, green top hat, green scarf and Irishman's pipe. "I'll send you the eighty bucks, sir," he yelled, giving the word *sir* its old infuriating touch.

Brubaker didn't care if the captain was watching. He grabbed the disgraced man's hand and said, "Take care of yourself, Mike. Pilots need you."

"I go for rough duty," Mike yelled, clutching his hat as the lines started to draw him over to the destroyer. "Because I really hate communists."

The chair dipped perilously toward the sea but Mike kept his legs clear. Instinctively the pilots cheered but the Irishman yelled derisively, "You apes go into the drink, not me!"

The new helicopter pilot was an officer, a college kid and no doubt competent, but the jet men and propeller crews knew that flying off the *Savo* would be a little tougher now.

The fear that was reborn when Brubaker watched Cag dive into the valley at Toko-ri grew all that day, augmented by the gloom of Mike Forney's dismissal and the briefing. After dinner, in the crowded ready room, the intelligence officer had passed around marked copies of the photographs made that morning and said, "Take-off at 0900. By then the sun will have driven ground fog out of the valley. Keep well south of the guns at Majon-ni. Cag, you tell them about the approach."

Cag, cigar in mouth, said briefly, "On paper it looks like a lot of flak concentrated here." He jabbed at the map with his right forefinger. "But it's not accurate. We'll go in low. We'll go in three times. And we'll go in from the east each time. When we're through, there won't be any more bridges."

There were some questions and then Cag handed them the cold dope. He held his cigar in his left hand and said, "Marty, you take your four men in at 1000 feet to suppress flak. I'll follow with my four at 1200. Brubaker, you mop up."

Tightly Brubaker gripped the arms of his chair and fought back his fear. He couldn't fly this mission. He couldn't take his jet inside that blazing rim of hills. His old bitterness at having been called back into service sneaked up into his throat and corroded his courage. Frantically, as if afraid he might break down before his peers, he rose and hurried out.

Stumbling down the narrow passageways of the carrier, he banged against stanchions and bruised his shin upon the damnable hatches. Seeking out his own room he slammed the door shut and climbed up into his bed under the steam pipes. In uncontrolled panic, there in the dark room, he cast about for some way to avoid the strike against the bridges.

"I'll go see the doc. I'll just walk in and announce, 'I've lost my nerve.'" Impulsively he climbed down and started for the door. Then he stopped and laughed nervously at himself.

For the navy had worked out the perfect way to handle situations like this. Suppose you went in and said you were too jittery to fly, the doc simply said, "OK. Don't fly." It was so easy that a man thought a hundred thousand times before he used that dodge. He stood alone, sweating, in his dark room and recalled the Cag's flight into the valley, and almost without knowing it he uttered the tricky words that bind a man to duty, those simple words that send men in jet planes against overwhelmingly protected bridges: "If Cag can fly that flak, so can I." That was what kept the navy system working. You could weasel out any time, but within the essence of your conscience lived the memory of other men no less afraid than you who were willing to tackle the dirty jobs. So you stuck.

But then a late flight returned and he thought ungraciously,

"What mission did they draw? Rail cuts. Up where there are no guns. Why don't they get the bridges? Why does it have to be me?"

He felt ashamed of himself and turned on the light but was appalled by his own gray and ashen face in the mirror. "Get hold of yourself!" he commanded. Methodically, as if attention to some one job would restore his courage, he sat down to write a letter to his wife, but after he had written only a few lines he drew back in disgust. "You stinker!" he whispered at his picture in the mirror. "Scaring Nancy by letting her know you expect to be killed at the bridges."

He began a new letter and with great composure told Nancy how much he loved the children and of how he longed for the days of peace when they could all go camping again in the Rockies back of Denver. He ended with a paragraph in which he described in detail the suit she had worn that day on the quay at Yokosuka. "It looked very expensive," he wrote, "and I was amazed when you said you made it yourself."

But when he crawled back into bed things were worse than before and like a stabbing agony in the darkness he cried, "Why does it have to be me?" He remembered the men he had known in Colorado. Some hated their wives but they stayed home. Others hated their jobs, but they stayed on those jobs. Some of them, he recalled, had always wanted to travel, some had loved airplanes, others were always picking a fight and some good Catholics like Mike Forney hated communism so much they could taste it. Others were poor and needed navy pay. But all of them stayed home.

Through the long night Brubaker wrestled with his fear. Toward morning he was taken with frenzy and leaped from bed, rushing down the passageway to report his loss of nerve, but he never reached the doctor. A shattering sound halted him and in the gloomy darkness he whispered, "They're launching the dawn planes. It won't be long now." Then the catapult fired again and he remembered something Forney had once said and he stumbled down the ladder to the port catapult room, breaking in among the crew and crying, "Where did Mike Forney stand?"

"Here."

"Is that the piston he told me about?"

"Yep."

Before Brubaker could ask more questions the engine fired and from its nest forward eleven tons of gleaming metal roared back with appalling force to stop a few inches from his face. Involuntarily he stumbled backward. The enlisted men laughed.

"Forney stood stock still," they said.

Mike had explained that he came to the catapult room whenever his nerves were getting tight and the explosion of that enormous piston right into his face cured him: "If a guy can take that, he can take anything," Mike had said, but before Brubaker got set the monstrous machine fired again and that tremendous gleaming force sprang at him. He fell back.

"Takes a real idiot to stay put," a crewman shouted.

"You ever tried it?" Brubaker asked.

"I ain't no idiot."

Brubaker rooted himself to a position from which he could not be budged, and like a frightened bullfighter he mumbled to himself, "This time I keep my feet here." While he watched, the mighty piston leaped at him, then stopped with a powerful uuuuush less than four inches from his face.

The catapult crew applauded and said, "Pretty soon now you'll be as crazy as Forney."

"Is that bad?" Brubaker asked. Briskly he returned through the darkened ship and climbed into bed. "Well," he assured himself, "at least I'm not yellow." But immediately he was more afraid: "Because you know the catapult's got to stop. But the guns at Toko-ri never do."

So when the messenger called at 0700 he found Brubaker awake and sweating, staring at the steam pipes. When he reported to the wardroom bleary-eyed, Cag asked, "What were you doing in the catapult room last night?"

There was no use kidding anybody so he replied, "I was jittery."

"Does sticking your face in a piston cure that?"

"Yes."

Cag knew he should have left it at that but this mission was too important so he asked, "You want to ground yourself? Because today we've got to do a first-rate professional job."

"That's what I'm here for."

"Good. I put you in the follow-through spot because I know that if my gang misses the bridges, you'll get 'em."

"I'm going to."

At 0730 the pilots moved into the cold ready room where the worst part of the flight took place. Twelve reasonably trim lithe young athletes began to pile onto themselves such a mass of encumbrances that soon they waddled like pigs, completely muscle bound and sweating from every pore. Sometimes even the bravest pilots felt their nerves shiver when they faced the degrading job of dressing for a winter flight.

Brubaker started in shorts. First he climbed into long-handled woolen underwear, then into a skin-tight g-suit, which applied pressure on vital parts of his body so that when he pulled out of steep dives the enormous drag of gravity, the g's, would not suck all the blood from his head. He covered the g-suit with inch-thick quilted underwear, two pairs of short bulky socks and a third which reached his knees. Then came the rough part, for even though the watertight rubber poopy suit had already saved his life once, getting into it was always murder.

Since the neck band had to be tight to keep out freezing water and since no zippers were allowed, he had to get into the poopy suit in a special way. A long slash ran from the left shoulder across the chest and down to the right hip and he climbed in through this hole, pushing his feet down into the massive boots and his head up through the impossibly tight neck band. Then he grabbed the two flaps of extra rubber along the slash and rolled them together into a bulky, watertight seal which fattened him like a watermelon. And as soon as he closed this final seal he began to sweat like a pig and every minute he wore the poopy suit he was smelly and wet and uncomfortable. From time to time he pulled the neck band out and blew fresh air inside to get some relief. That's why the ready room was kept so cold, to keep the pilots from sweating, but all the same they sweated.

After the poopy suit came the survival vest, the pistol, the bulky Mae West, the hip knife, three cumbersome pairs of gloves, golden crash helmet, oxygen connection, harness straps and heavy goggles.

Weighed down like some primeval monster, he waddled to the escalator which lifted him to the flight deck—another trick to keep down sweat—where an enlisted man handed him the board for clamping onto his knee with navigation data, codes, plots and all kinds of miscellaneous papers.

Even when he climbed into his jet there was more gear, so complicated that his plane captain had to crouch behind him and adjust safety belt, shoulder harness, ejection gear, microphone cord and oxygen supply. Harry Brubaker, who was about to soar into space with a freedom no previous men in history had known, was loaded down with such intolerable burdens that at times he felt he must suffocate; just as many citizens of his world, faced with a chance at freedoms never before dreamed of, felt so oppressed by modern problems and requirements that they were sure they must collapse.

As Brubaker adjusted himself to the cockpit he was hemmed in on left and right by more than seventy-five switches and controls. Directly facing him were sixteen instruments and thirteen more switches. He thought, "If there were one more thing to do . . ." He never finished the sentence for the mighty catapult fired and he was shot into space, where the suffocating paraphernalia and the maze of switches seemed to fall away and he roared into the upper blue, tied down only by his cancerous fear of the bridges at Toko-ri.

But today he would not see those bridges, for at Wonsan the radio crackled and he heard Cag's disappointed voice, "Weather scout reports target closed in. Ground fog. Stand by for alternate instructions."

When Brubaker heard this life-saving news he shouted, "A reprieve! I knew I wasn't meant to tackle the bridges today." He started to sing the chorus of *Cielito Lindo* but stopped in embarrassment when he saw that in his surging joy he had unconsciously lifted his Banshee 400 feet higher than the formation.

But ground fog did not save him, for in the next minute a miracle of modern war occurred. Cag received a radio message from Admiral Tarrant, and instantly the twelve jets stopped in midflight, almost as if they were a flock of pheasant searching for a Colorado grain field. Abruptly they turned south, heading for the mountainous battle front, where in the trenches a new emergency had arisen.

At dawn that morning a battalion of South Korean infantry had been hit by a murderous concentration of communist power and it became apparent that the Koreans would be annihilated unless air support could be provided. So a United States army liaison officer serving at the front phoned a Korean general, who called the United States army command in Seoul, who got hold of an air force general, who said he had no planes but would try to get some from a marine general, who suggested that Admiral Tarrant, far out to sea, might have some to spare. The inquiry arrived in flag plot just as the early-morning weather plane was reporting: "Toko-ri closed in but good. Takusan ground fog. Takusan no see."

Tarrant, who normally would not see such a message, made a note to chew out a pilot who would use Japanese in a battle report, and replied, "One flight of twelve heavily armed jets available. Already airborne."

Seoul immediately ordered, "Proceed Roundelay. Operate as he directs."

So by means of field telephone, radio, ship-to-shore communication and ship-to-plane, American jets were diverted to rescue South Korean foot soldiers. As the planes swept south Cag called ahead, "Roundelay, twelve jets reporting for orders. We're loaded."

From the bright morning sky came a whispery voice: "This is Roundelay. I'm flying an SNJ."

Each jet pilot was astonished that in today's swift war the out-of-date old SNJ would still be used. It had been ancient before they took basic training, but no one had quite the shock that Harry Brubaker experienced. "An SNJ?" he repeated incredulously and he was back in 1935, a gangling boy stretched out upon the floor, quietly and supremely happy, for he had mailed the box tops and the company had kept its promise. Here was the highly colored put-together of America's latest plane. "It was an SNJ," he recalled.

Then suddenly from behind a mountain, there was the real SNJ, a rickety, two-bladed propeller job with a high greenhouse, a useless spare seat and six smoke rockets slung precariously under its wings. A slap-happy air force captain was wheeling it slowly around and Harry thought, "What's an SNJ doing here?" Then he learned.

"This is Roundelay. Get the big guns first."

"Can't see 'em," Cag said.

"Follow me."

And to the amazement of the jet pilots Roundelay trundled his slow plane down almost to the treetops and delivered a smoke rocket against the target. "See it now?" he called.

"Will do!" Cag cried, and he led his twelve screaming jets into a howling dive, right onto the gun and it fired no more.

"Strictly wonderful," Roundelay called. "D'you see the other two?"

"Negative."

"Watch this smoke." And the buglike SNJ hopped almost at ground level up a narrow valley to deliver another smoke rocket against another gun. Then, when it seemed the midget plane must follow the rocket against the rocks, the pilot twisted free, skipped over a ridge and ducked down upon a third gun.

"Will do!" Cag reported, and when his swift jets had silenced the guns, Roundelay called cheerily, "You must come back often."

The jets had zoomed so high they could not keep track of the tiny plane, but then sunlight glinted on the ridiculous greenhouse and they heard Roundelay call, "I think I see Red troops beginning a new attack. Follow me." And once more he hurried off like a busy old woman going to market.

Brubaker's division was aloft and he watched Cag's four jets roar low into a column of communists assaulting a hill. With appalling accuracy the Banshees spread their hundred pound bombs, each wound with high-tension steel wire that shattered into small pieces with machine gun fury. The communist advance wavered.

"Next division," Roundelay called. "Keep hitting them while they're confused."

"Will do," Brubaker replied, but as he prepared for his dive, the SNJ wheeled suddenly and Roundelay called, "Do you see what I see?"

Below, in obedience to some order of incredible stupidity, more than one hundred communists had moved out of a woods and onto a frozen road, and as Brubaker's jets came screaming at them they did an even more unbelievable thing. They fell to their knees in the middle of the road, clasped their arms about their heads and made no effort to escape inevitable death. The tactic so astonished Brubaker that he gasped, "They're sitting ducks!" And some ancient boyhood training in the mountains back of Denver restrained him.

But when he had zoomed high into the heavens he heard the unemotional voice of Roundelay: "Clobber those guys. That's their standard trick. Throwing you off balance."

So the jets wheeled and came screaming back down the road. Not a communist moved. Not one hit the ditch. They huddled and waited. "Here it comes," Brubaker whispered grimly, and his finger pressed the trigger. Keeping his eye upon the kneeling troops, he watched his bullets spray a path among them. "You wanted trouble," he said weakly.

Roundelay now spotted another column of attacking communists and called in Cag's division. Brubaker, with sickening detachment, watched the merciless jets and thought, "Those people in Denver who ridicule air force reports of enemy dead ought to see this." And he remembered Admiral Tarrant's words: "If we keep enough planes over them enough hours somebody's got to get hurt. And when they hurt bad enough, they'll quit."

"How's your fuel?" Roundelay asked.

"Can do one more pass," Cag replied, and the jet pilots, who approached the speed of sound, watched as the slow little doodlebug SNJ hopped about in search of fat targets. Brubaker, pulling out of his last bombing run, sped past the prop plane and for an instant of suspended time the two men looked casually at each other. Harry saw that the air force man was very thin and wore a moustache but he saw no more, for a five-inch communist gun, hidden until then, fired one lucky shot and blew the frail little SNJ completely to ribbons.

In terrible fury Brubaker launched his jet at the gun and tried to root it from its cave. He carried his fire almost into the muzzle of the enemy gun. Then, although his fuel was getting tight, he turned and made another run, pushing his jet to a deadly speed. He saw the gun, saw the wounded crew and the shell casings. On he came, firing until his own guns were silent, and the communists fell away. Then he zoomed aloft to overtake the homeward jets, but except for his wingman the planes were far away.

"You ought to tell me when you're going to run wild," the wingman protested.

"I really clobbered that one," Brubaker said grimly, but as the two Banshees soared away from the ravaged battleground with its wrecked artillery and dead bodies huddled along frozen roads, the enemy gun that Brubaker thought he had destroyed resumed firing. Mute with outrage, Brubaker wanted to dive upon it once more but he heard his wingman say, "Their side has guts, too."

Finally, when the roar of battle was past and the jets were far in the wintry sky Brubaker called, "How's your fuel?"

"Thousand five."

His own gauge read just under a thousand and he thought, "I hope Beer Barrel is bringing us in." Then he heard his wingman cry, "There's Cag, up ahead."

The two jets increased speed to rejoin the flight and all pilots began the difficult job of trying to spot the task force. Drifting clouds mottled the sea and made the ships almost invisible, but they had to be within a small area, for to the east hung the permanent snow line and to the north a new storm boxed in the fleet, but no one could see the ships.

It was ridiculous. Twelve highly-trained pilots couldn't find a task force of nineteen ships, including carriers, cruisers and a battleship. For some perverse reason Brubaker took delight in this limitation of human beings and thought, "You never master this business." Then Cag called, "There's home!" and where absolutely nothing had been visible a moment before the jet pilots saw the nineteen ships. And Brubaker, seeing them as big as barns on an open meadow, laughed.

But his relief didn't last because when the jets descended he saw that the carrier deck was pitching rather formidably, and this meant many wave-offs because the landing officer would have to wait until the carrier stabilized itself between lurches, so that you might approach in perfect altitude but find the deck in a momentary trough and have to go round again. That took fuel. Because when you got a wave-off you had to pour it on. And there went your fuel.

Then he had a happy thought: "They probably haven't turned into the wind. The deck'll be better when they do."

But as he watched, a flight of jets took off from the *Hornet* and that proved the carriers were already into the wind, so he looked at the heaving *Savo*, stern leaping high in the air, bow down and said, "There's your deck and you'll like it." Then, although he never prayed, he mumbled, "Beer Barrel, be out there today!" And as if in answer to this plea Cag announced, "Beer Barrel's bringing us in on a pitching deck. Anybody short on fuel?"

Brubaker reported, "1591 reporting over ship with 800."

He listened to Cag forward this news to the *Savo* and then call, "We'll double up. No trouble getting aboard."

So instead of the normal interval which would enable one jet to land each 26 seconds, the twelve Banshees formed a tight little circle yielding 15-second intervals so that whenever the deck stabilized there would be some jet diving right for it. But this also meant that one out of every two planes would have to take automatic wave-offs. "Hope I'm one of the lucky ones," Brubaker said.

He was. On his outward leg the *Savo* pitched so badly that no landing plane got aboard, but by the time Harry's downward leg started, the big ship was shuddering into stabilized position. "It'll hold that position for at least a minute," Brubaker assured himself. "Time to get three of us aboard." Nervously he ticked off the jets ahead of him in the circle. "Seven of them. Just right. First two will have to pass because the deck won't be steady enough, but three, five and seven'll make it. Boy, I'm seven!"

Then he saw Beer Barrel's paddles bringing number three in and the deck crew had the hook disengaged in two and a half seconds and the deck was steady and clear. "What an outfit when the going's tough," Brubaker said admiringly.

Then hell broke loose. The pilot in jet number five did what Beer Barrel had warned his men never to do. As his Banshee neared the cut-off point the deck lurched and the pilot tried to compensate. Instead of flying Beer Barrel he flew the deck and missed every wire. In great panic he managed to pancake into the barriers but he ripped them both away and the crucial barricade as well.

Brubaker, screaming over the wreckage, saw instantly that it would be many minutes before the deck could be cleared and he cried feverishly to himself, "I don't want to go into the sea again."

His fear was unreasonable. He could see the helicopters waiting to rescue him. He saw the alert destroyers, always quick to lift a downed pilot from the waves. But he also saw the gray sea and he'd been down there once. "The second time you crack up. You sink and they never find you." Instinctively he felt to see if his three gloves were watertight at the wrist. That's where the sea crept in and froze you. Then he pulled his hand away in horror and whispered, "Beer Barrel, don't let me go into the drink."

Then he got hold of himself and heard Cag's quiet voice say, "All nylon torn away. At least ten minutes to repair it. Is that critical for 1591?"

Brubaker breathed deeply to drive down any quiver in his voice and reported evenly, "I'm down to 600."

Cag said to the ship, "1591 low on fuel. Must land on first pass after barrier is fixed."

The radio said, "*Hornet's* deck temporarily fouled. But would landing there in eight minutes be of help?"

Promptly Brubaker said, "I'd waste just as much gas getting in the circle. I'll stick here." What he did not say was that without Beer Barrel's help he might lose his nerve completely.

With mounting fear he noticed that the crashed plane still fouled up the landing space and the broken barriers were not being promptly repaired. What made this especially infuriating was that all this time the carrier remained in stabilized position and all the jets could have been landed. Then he saw something that froze him. The towering black crane called Tilly was being moved into position alongside the wrecked Banshee, right where the missing nylon barricade should have been. Then a quiet, reassuring voice spoke to him, offering a choice. "1591," the impersonal voice said, "*Hornet's* deck still not ready. Impossible to erect barricade in time for you to land but we must protect planes parked forward. Have therefore moved Tilly into position to stop you positively in case you miss wire. Do you wish to attempt deck landing or do you wish to ditch? Advise."

He stared down at the monstrous crane looming up from the middle of the deck. "That'll stop me. Oh boy, will that stop me!" It was a brutal thing to do, to move Tilly out there, but he appreciated why it had been done. Behind the crane were parked $40,000,000 worth of aircraft and they must be protected and he felt no resentment at the maneuver. But before replying he reasoned carefully, "The last guy missed the wires because the deck pitched. I can too," and he was about to elect ditching but a compelling instinct told him that his only hope for safety lay with Beer Barrel.

"I'm coming in," he said.

He made his first turn and prayed, "Beer Barrel, bring me in. I don't care if the deck is going crazy, bring me in."

On the down-wind leg he dropped to correct altitude and avoided looking at the pitching deck. He kept his eyes on the screen that shielded Beer Barrel from the wind but for a moment he became quite sick, for the stern was bouncing about like a derelict rowboat.

"Bring me in, Beer Barrel."

Then as he whipped into the final turn he saw that terrible thing, the crane Tilly filling the end of the landing space and he would have turned aside had he not also seen Beer Barrel. The big man stood on one foot, his paddles up . . . still good . . . still coming . . . oh, Beer Barrel, keep me coming. . . .

Then mercifully the cut sign, the firm hook catching securely, the run of singing wire, the tremendous pull upon his shoulders, and his eyes looking up at the monstrous crane into which he did not crash.

From the flag bridge Admiral Tarrant followed the emergency landing and when he saw Brubaker lunge onto the deck safely he sent an aide to bring the pilot to him as soon as intelligence had checked battle reports. Some minutes later the young man appeared relaxed and smiling in freshly pressed khaki and said, "Somebody told me there were eight hundred ways to get back aboard a carrier. Any one of them's good, if you make it."

Tarrant laughed, jabbed a cup of coffee into the pilot's hands and asked casually, "What were you doing in the catapult room last night?"

Brubaker sat down carefully, sipped his coffee and said, "I lost my nerve last night."

"You looked pretty steady out there just now."

It was very important now that Brubaker say just the right thing, for he knew that something big was eating the admiral but he couldn't guess what, so he looked over the rim of his cup and said, "Best sedative in the world is Beer Barrel and those paddles."

The admiral remained standing, somewhat annoyed at Brubaker's having presumed to sit. Nevertheless, the bonds of sympathy which bound him to the younger man were at work. He didn't want Brubaker to participate in the attack on the bridges, so in an offhand manner he asked, "Son, do you want me to ground you . . . for tomorrow's flight against Toko-ri?"

Brubaker thought, "If he'd wanted me to stay down he wouldn't have asked. He'd have told me. This way he hopes I won't accept." But of his own will and regardless of the admiral he decided to say no and replied evenly, "If anybody goes, I go."

Admiral Tarrant was at once aware that he had posed his question the wrong way and said, "I think you're jittery, son. I think you ought to stay down."

Again Brubaker thought, "The old man's wrestling with himself. He wants to ground me but he's afraid it would look like favoritism. So he's trying to trick me into asking. That way everything would be OK." But again he said, "I want to fly against the bridges."

Certain, and in some ways pleased, that the young man would refuse the order, Tarrant said, "Harry, I've been watching you. There's nothing shameful in a man's reaching the end of his rope for the time being. You know I consider you our finest pilot . . . after the squadron leaders. But I can't let you fly tomorrow."

And Brubaker said quietly, "Sir, if you'd offered me this chance last night I'd have jumped to accept it. Or half an hour ago when I stared at that big black Tilly. But I think you know how it is, sir. Any time you get back safe, that day's trembling is over. Right now I haven't a nerve. Look." He held out his coffee saucer and it remained rigid.

"You're sure it's passed?"

"Positive. Remember when you told my wife about the voluntary men who save the world? I've seen two of these men. It shakes you to the roots of your heart to see such men in action."

"Who'd you see?" Tarrant asked, the sparring over.

"Yesterday I saw Cag take his photographic plane. . . ."

"Cag?"

"Yes, sir. I saw a man so brave. . . . Admiral, he went in so low that he simply had to get knocked down. Then he went in again . . . lower."

"Cag?" Admiral Tarrant repeated, amazed.

"And this morning . . . Did anyone tell you about the air force spotter in the SNJ?"

"No."

Brubaker's voice almost broke but he stammered, "He was killed by a gun I might have knocked out . . . if I'd really been on the ball." There was a long silence in which Tarrant poured more coffee. Finally Brubaker said, "Sometimes you look honor right in the face. In the face of another man. It's terrifying." His voice trailed away and he added in a whisper, "So I have no choice. I have to go out tomorrow. If he could fly an SNJ, I can fly a jet." He laughed nervously and thrust his saucer out again. It remained immovable, like the end of a solid stone arm. "No nerves now," he said.

It was 1145 next morning when Cag, his jets poised aloft for their first run against the bridges, cried, "Attack, attack, attack!"

With deadly precision, and ignoring the mortal curtain of communist fire, four Banshees assigned to flak-suppression flung themselves upon the heaviest guns at more than 500 miles an hour. Rendezvousing to the north, they swept back in ghostly blue streaks and raked the principal emplacements a second time, but as they reached the middle of this passage communist fire struck number three plane and with a violence few men have witnessed it smashed into a hill and exploded in an instantaneous orange flash.

Before the eight pilots aloft could realize what had happened Cag called quietly, "Prepare to attack," and the four jets in his division peeled off for swift assault upon the bridges. They descended at an angle steeper than 50° and for the entire final run of two miles no pilot swerved or dodged until his first huge bomb sped free.

From aloft Brubaker saw that Cag had got two of the bridges. Now he must finish the job. He brought his division down in a screaming dive, aware that when he straightened out the pull of gravity upon him would suck the blood away from his head and drag his lips into grotesque positions, but the fascination of those looming bridges of Toko-ri lured him on. Lower and lower he came. When he finally pickled his bomb and pulled away he absorbed so many g's that a heaviness came upon his legs and his face was drawn drowsily down upon his chin. But he knew nothing of this for he experienced only surging elation. He had bombed the bridges.

Then he heard the dismal voice: "No damage to main bridge."

And you had to believe that voice, for it was Roy's, last man through. Tomorrow stateside newspapers might exaggerate the damage. You could kid the intelligence officer. And you could lie like a schoolboy to pilots from another squadron, but last man through told the truth. No damage.

"I'm sure Brubaker got a span," Cag argued.

"Negative," Roy replied flatly.

"How about the truck bridges?"

"Clobbered, clobbered, clobbered."

Cag called, "Stand by for run number two," and eleven jets orbited for position. The three flak-suppression Banshees stampeded for the gun-rimmed valley and as they roared in the leader confirmed Roy's report: "No damage to the main bridge." But the last of the flak jets reported, "We really have the ground fire slowed down."

Then, to the surprise of the communists, Cag brought his men in over the same check points as before and cheated some of the communist gunners, who had been gambling that he would use the other entrance to their valley. Through gray bomb smoke and bursts of flak, through spattering lead and their own fears, the first four pilots bore in upon the bridges. Roaring straight down the railroad track like demon trains they pickled their heavy freight upon the bridge and pulled away with sickening g's upon them, their mouths gaping wide like idiots, their eyes dulled with war and the pull of gravity.

As Brubaker led his men upon the bridges he saw a magnificent sight. Three spans were down and a fourth was crumbling. The two truck bridges were demolished and the alternate railroad span was in the mud. In triumph he called, "This is Brubaker. All bridges down. Divert to the dump." And with blood perilously withdrawn from his head he swung his Banshee away from the bridges, over a slight rise of ground, and down upon the sprawling military dumps. Strafing, bombing, twisting, igniting, he screamed on, his three teammates following. Somebody's bomb struck ammunition. Consecutive explosions, each keeping the next alive, raced through the stores.

This time Roy, last man through, said, "We hit something big." Cag, aloft called, "All planes, all planes. Work over the dump."

Brubaker, now higher than the others, watched the dazzling procession of Banshees. Swooping low, they spun their fragmentation bombs earthward and retired into the lonely distance. Returning, they dodged hills and spread deathly fire. Over snowy ridges they formed for new runs and wherever they moved there was silent beauty and the glint of sunlight on the bronzed helmet of some man riding beneath the plexiglas canopy. It was a fearsome thing to watch jets assume control of this valley where the bridges had been, and it was gloomy, for no matter where any of the pilots looked they could see the scarred hillside against which one of their team had plunged to death a few minutes before.

His ammunition nearly spent, Brubaker nosed down for a final run upon the spattered dumps, but Cag called, "Stay clear of the ammo dumps. We have them popping there." So he twisted his jet to the south, away from the ammo but before he could launch his dive, two jets streaked across his target and jettisoned their bombs so that again he had to pull away. He was tempted to drop his last bomb where he thought he saw a gun emplacement but promptly he discarded this idea as unworthy for it occurred to him, quite clearly in this instant of decision, that even one bomb more might mean significant interdiction of supplies to the front: fewer bullets for communist gunners, fewer blankets for their trenches, less food. He recalled Admiral Tarrant's words: "If we keep the pressure high enough something's got to explode over there."

So in an effort to add that extra degree of pressure which might help to beat back aggression, he turned away from his easy target and picked out a supply dump. He activated his nose guns and watched their heavy bullets rip into valued cargo and set it afire. Then he resolutely pickled his last bomb but as he pulled out of his dive, with heavy g's upon his face, he heard a pinking-thud.

"I've been hit!" he cried and as the jet sped upward chaos took over. He lost control of his mind and of the thundering Banshee and in panic thought only of Wonsan harbor. He felt the irresistible lure of the sea where friendly craft might rescue him and violently he wrenched his nose toward the east and fled homeward like a sea-stricken thing. But as soon as he had made this desperate turn he became aware that panic was flying the plane, not he, and he called quietly, "Joe, Joe. Just took a hit. So far I'm all right."

From the dark sky aloft came the reassuring whisper, "Harry, this is Joe. I have you in sight."

"Joe, drop down and look me over."

Now an ugly vibration identified itself as coming from the port engine but for one fragile second of time it seemed as if the frightening sound might abate. Then, with shattering echoes, the entire engine seemed to fall apart and Brubaker whispered to himself, "I'm not going to get this crate out of Korea."

A communist bullet no bigger than a man's thumb, fired at random by some ground defender of the dump, had blundered haphazardly into the turbine blades, which were then whirring at nearly 13,000 revolutions a minute. So delicately was the jet engine balanced that the loss of only two blade tips had thrown the entire mechanism out of balance, and the grinding noise Brubaker heard was the turbine throwing off dozens of knifelike blades which slashed into the fuselage or out through the dark sky. Like the society which had conceived the engine, the turbine was of such advanced construction that even trivial disruption of one fundamental part endangered the entire structure.

He had, of course, immediately cut fuel to the damaged engine and increased revolutions on the other and as soon as the clatter of the damaged turbines subsided he cut off its air supply and eliminated the destructive vibrations altogether. Then, in fresh silence, he checked the twenty principal indicators on his panel and found things to be in pretty good shape. "I might even make it back to the ship," he said hopefully. But promptly he discarded this for a more practical objective: "Anyway, I'll be able to reach the sea."

He laughed at himself and said, "Look at me! Yesterday I

pushed the panic button because I might have to go into the sea. Today I reached for it because I might miss the water."

As he reasoned with himself Joe came lazily out from beneath his wing and waved. "Everything all right now?" Joe asked.

"All under control," he answered.

"Fuel OK?"

"Fine. More than 2,000 pounds."

"Keep checking it," Joe said quietly. "You may be losing a little."

Then the sick panic returned and no more that day would it leave. Impeded by heavy gear he tried to look aft but couldn't. Straining himself he saw fleetingly from the corner of his eye a thin wisp of white vapor trailing in the black sky. Knocking his goggles away he tried to look again and his peripheral vision spied the dusty vapor, no thicker than a pencil.

"Joe," he called quietly. "That looks like a fuel leak."

"Don't your gauges show it?"

"Don't seem to."

"You'll make the sea all right," Joe said, and both men surrendered any idea of the ship.

"I'll make the sea," Harry said.

"I'll trail you," Joe called.

In a few minutes he said, "You're losing fuel pretty fast, Harry."

There was no longer any use to kid himself. "Yeah. Now the instruments show it."

Joe drew his slim blue jet quite close to Harry's and the two men looked at one another as clearly as if they had been across a table in some bar. "I still think you'll make the sea," Joe said.

But Harry knew that merely reaching the sea wasn't enough. "How far out must we go in Wonsan harbor to miss the communist mines?" he asked.

Joe ruffled through some papers clipped to his knee and replied, "You ought to go two miles. But you'll make it, Harry."

The turbine blade that had sliced into the fuel line now broke loose and allowed a heavy spurt of gasoline to erupt so that Joe could clearly see it. "You're losing gas pretty fast now," he said.

There was a sad drop on the fuel gauge and Harry said, "Guess that does it."

To prevent explosion, he immediately killed his good engine and felt the Banshee stutter in midair, as if caught by some enormous hand. Then, at 250 miles an hour, he started the long and agonizing glide which carried him ever nearer to the sea and always lower toward the mountains.

Quickly Joe cut his own speed and said, "We better call the word."

With crisp voice Brubaker announced the strange word which by general consent across the world has come to mean disaster. In Malaya, in China, over Europe or in the jungle airports of the Amazon this word betokens final catastrophe: "Mayday, Mayday."

It was heard by communist monitors and by the officers in Task Force 77. Aloft, Cag heard it and turned his jets back to keep watch upon their stricken member. And aboard the scow the newly reported helicopter team of Mike Forney and Nestor Gamidge heard it.

"Mayday, Mayday."

Silently, through the upper reaches of the sky, the two men flew side by side. They had never been particularly friendly, for their interests and ages varied, nor had they talked much, but now in the dark violet sky with sunlight gleaming beneath them on the hills of Korea they began their last urgent conversation, their faces bright in plexiglas and their voices speaking clear through the vast emptiness of the space.

"We'll make the sea," Joe said reassuringly.

"I'm sure going to try."

They drifted down to the sunny spaces of the sky, into the region of small cloud and laughing shadow and Joe asked, "Now when we reach the sea will you parachute or ditch?"

"I ditched once, I'll do it again."

"I never asked you, how does the Banshee take the water?"

"Fine, if you keep the tail down."

"Remember to jettison your canopy, Harry."

"I don't aim to be penned in."

"Six more minutes will put us there."

So they fought to the sea. As if caught in the grip of some atavistic urge that called them back to the safety of the sea after the millions of years during which men had risen from this element, these two pilots nursed their jets away from inhospitable land and out toward the open sea. They were low now and could spot communist villages and from time to time they saw bursts of communist guns, so they fought to reach the sea.

But they did not make it. For looming ahead of them rose the hills in back of Wonsan harbor. Between the jets and the sea stood these ugly hills and there was no way to pass them. Instinctively Harry shoved the throttle forward to zoom higher—only a couple of hundred feet, even fifty might do—but relentlessly the stricken Banshee settled lower.

From the adjoining plane Joe pointed to the obstructing hills and Harry said, "I see them. I won't make it."

Joe asked, "Now, Harry, are you going to jump or crash land!"

"Crash," Harry said promptly. Back in the States he had decided to stick with his plane no matter what happened. Besides, communists shot at parachutes, whereas the speed of a crash often took them by surprise and permitted rescue operations.

"Keep your wheels up," Joe said.

"Will do."

"Be sure to hit every item on the check-off list."

"Will do."

"Harry, make sure those shoulder straps are really tight."

"Already they're choking me."

"Good boy. Now, Harry, remember what happened to Lou. Unhook your oxygen mask and radio before you hit."

"Will do."

"Knife? Gun?"

Harry nodded. Although he was soon going to hit some piece of Korean ground at a speed of 130 miles, his plane bursting out of control at impact, in this quiet preparatory moment he could smile out of his canopy and converse with Joe as if they were long-time friends reviewing a basketball game.

"Pretty soon now," he said.

"I'll move ahead and try to find a good field," Joe said. Before he pulled away he pointed aloft and said, "Cag's upstairs."

Soon he called, "This field looks fair."

"Isn't that a ditch running down the middle?"

"Only shadows."

"You think I can stop short of the trees?"

"Easy, Harry. Easy."

"Well then, that's our field."

"Listen, Harry. When you do land, no matter what happens, get out fast."

"You bet. I don't like exploding gas."

"Good boy. Remember, fellow. Fast. Fast."

Desperately Brubaker wanted to make one run along the field to check things for himself, but the remorseless glide kept dragging him down and he heard Joe's patient voice calling, "Harry, you better jettison that canopy right now."

"I forgot."

Like a schoolteacher with a child Joe said, "That was first on the check-off list. Did you hit those items, Harry?"

"I got them all," Harry said.

"Field look OK?"

"You pick 'em real good, son."

Those were the last words Harry said to his wingman, for the ground was rushing up too fast and there was much work to do. Dropping his right wing to make the turn onto the field, he selected what looked like the clearest strip and lowered his flaps. Then, kicking off a little altitude by means of a side slip, he headed for the earth. Tensed almost to the shattering point, he held the great Banshee steady, tail down, heard a ripping sound, saw his right wing drop suddenly and tear away, watched a line of trees rush up at him and felt the final tragic collapse of everything. The impact almost tore the harness through his left shoulder socket but without this bracing he would surely have been killed. For an instant he thought the pain might make him faint, but the rich sweet smell of gasoline reached him and with swift planned motions he ripped himself loose from the smoking plane. But when he started to climb down he realized that his oxygen supply tube and his radio were still connected, just as Joe had warned. Laughing at himself he said, "Some guys you can't tell anything." With a powerful lurch he broke the cords and leaped upon Korean soil.

He was in a rice field three miles from a village. Beyond lay other rice fields and many curious U-shaped houses of the Korean countryside, their roofs covered with snow. To the north were mountains, to the south a row of trees, while from the east came a hint of salt air telling him that the sea was not far distant. But even as he surveyed his field he started running clumsily from the plane and before he had run far it burst into flame and exploded with numerous small blasts which sent billows of smoke into the air, informing communists in the village that another American plane had crashed. "They'll be after me soon," he thought and ran faster.

Within a few steps he was soaked with sweat inside his poopy suit and his breath hurt as it fought its way into his lungs. But still he ran, his big boots sticking in snowy mud, his intolerable gear holding him back. Finally he had to rest and sat upon a mound of earth forming the bank of a wide ditch that ran along the western edge of the field, but when one foot went into the center of the ditch he drew back in disgust for the smell he stirred up told him this was used for storing sewage until it was placed upon the rice fields. The stench was great and he started to leave but across the field he saw two communist soldiers approach the burning jet with rifles. So he did not leave the ditch but hid behind the mound of earth and reached for the revolver which he had once fired nine times in practice. He inspected its unfamiliar construction and remembered that it contained six bullets, to which he could add the twelve sewed onto his holster straps. "None to waste," he said.

Then one of the soldiers shouted that he had discovered the American's trail in the snow. The two men stopped, pointed almost directly to where he hid and started for him, their rifles ready.

At first he thought he would try to run down the ditch and hide in the line of trees but he realized the soldiers would intercept him before he could accomplish that. So he decided to stick it out where he was, and he hefted his revolver, for American pilots knew that if they were captured in this part of Korea they were usually shot.

"I'll wait till they reach that spot," he said, indicating a muddy place. "Then I'll let 'em have it." It did not occur to him that he probably wouldn't be able to hit a man ten feet away and that the spot he had selected was ridiculously remote, but fortunately he was not called upon to learn this ugly lesson, for as the two soldiers approached the point at which he was determined to fire, Joe's Banshee whirled out of the noonday sun and blasted the communists. Then, with a wailing cry, it screamed to rendezvous with Cag for the flight back to the *Savo*.

From his filthy ditch, Harry watched the mysterious and lovely jet stream out to sea and cried, "I'd sure like to be going with you." They were supreme in the sky, these rare, beautiful things, slimlined, nose gently dipping, silver canopy shining in the sun. Once he had been part of those jets and now, huddling to earth, he was thankful that he had known the sweeping flight, the penetration of upper space, the roaring dive with g's making his face heavy like a lion's, and final exultant soaring back to unlimited reaches of the sky. Then, as they disappeared completely, he pictured them entering the landing circle and he thought, "It would be fun, heading in toward Beer Barrel right now." Then he dismissed the jets.

He was determined to find a better refuge before new communists arrived, for the smell in this ditch was becoming too strong to tolerate, but when he did start to run toward the trees he saw four people standing there. Quickly he brandished his revolver at them, but they must have known he could not shoot them from so far for they stood impassively watching.

They were the family from the nearest farm, a mother, father and two children, dressed in discarded uniforms and brandishing rakes. He stopped to see if they intended attacking him, but they remained still and he saw them not as Koreans but as the Japanese family that had intruded upon his sulphur bath that morning in the Fuji-san and an unbearable longing for his own wife and children possessed him and it was then—there in bright sunlight in the rice field—that he knew he would not see his family again.

He was driven from this brief reflection by the arrival of more soldiers. From the very trees to which he was heading appeared eleven guards, shouting in Korean, so he hastily dived back to his stinking ditch where they could not hit him. They launched a methodical encircling attack but before they could bring him under fire four F4U's appeared overhead, called in by Cag to protect the downed pilot until rescue operations could begin.

Using Brubaker as their focus point, the slow propeller planes established a four-leaf clover in which each flew a big figure eight with such perfect timing as to have one plane coming in over Brubaker at all times, with alternate planes commanding different sectors of land so that no enemy dare approach.

The very first run enabled the F4U men to spot the eleven communists, and with sharp fire they tied the soldiers down. In the respite Brubaker thought, "With such cover a helicopter might make it," and he began to hope. Then, thinking to find a better spot from which to dash to the copter if it should arrive, he started to move out, but the Korean family saw him and thought he was moving toward them, so they withdrew. The F4U man responsible for this sector spied the Koreans, saw their tattered uniforms and roared upon them, his guns ablaze.

"No!" Brubaker screamed.

"No! No! No!" He waved his arms, jumped wildly to divert the F4U.

But the pilot could not see him. Focusing his sights grimly at what he knew to be the enemy, he brought his fiery guns a few yards from the faces of the Korean family. For one ghastly moment he thought two of the soldiers might have been children, but by then he was far away, roaring back into the four-leafed clover.

Sick, Harry Brubaker stood in the ditch and thought of his own daughters, and his heavy body was cold with much sweat.

He was standing thus when the helicopter appeared. It had lumbered in from the scow, dodging ground fire and flying so low that a revolver bullet could have destroyed it. Smack in the middle of the rice field it landed and Mike Forney got out. He wore his green top hat, a new Baron von Richthofen scarf of Japanese silk and a carbine. Behind him stumbled sad-faced Nestor Gamidge, also with a carbine. Leaving Gamidge at the copter, Forney ran across the rice field shouting, "Relax, Harry! Everything's under control."

Brubaker shouted, "Better dodge and duck."

"Why, is there a war goin' on?"

"Look!" He pointed toward the trees and as he did so a volley of machine gun fire spattered the helicopter. Gamidge fell to the ground but rolled over several times and indicated that he was all right, but above his head the helicopter burst into flames.

Forney jumped into the ditch and turned back to watch the fire in silence. No other copter would come onto this field. With flames of noon in their eyes the two men in the ditch looked at each other, unable to speak. Then slowly Mike pulled his right foot up.

"Harry," he asked. "Is this what I think it is?"

"Yep."

Scornfully he said, "You sure picked a wonderful place to fight a war." Then he shrugged his shoulders and growled, "We might as well get Nestor in here. Three of us can stand those apes off for days."

He hefted his carbine nonchalantly and started across the rice field to convoy Gamidge but when the sallow-faced Kentuckian stood up, communist bullets chopped him in the chest and he fell. Mike, still wearing his green hat, blasted the line of trees in pathetic fury, for he must have known his carbine could not carry so far. Then he ran forward to where Nestor lay but soon he crawled back to the stinking ditch and tried not to look at Harry.

"Is he dead?"

"Yep."

In silence the two men tried to build protection for their faces, but when they reached into the ditch for stones, an evil smell arose, so that Forney stared back at the ditch and muttered, "I could have picked a better . . ." Then he said bitterly, "They were goin' to give Nestor a medal."

"Why'd you bring the copter in here, Mike?"

"I take care of my men, sir."

"How is it aboard the scow?" Brubaker phrased the question so as to imply that Forney would be returning there when this day was over.

"It's fair, but carrier duty spoils you."

"I liked the *Savo*," Brubaker said, and when referring to himself he used the completed tense, surrendering hope.

Forney caught this and said, "You know what kills me right now? Thinking of Kimiko going to bed with that ape from the *Essex*."

"That would be tough," Brubaker agreed.

The two men looked up at the F4U's and Forney asked, "How much longer will they be able to stay?"

"Not long," Harry replied.

"Well, we got nothin' to worry about. The jets'll be back."

Harry said, "This morning I had a chance to watch jets in action. They're terrific."

"Look at those apes," Mike said, pointing to where communists were starting to move in. From time to time accurate rifle fire pinked the top of the mound and Brubaker thought ruefully of people back in Denver who visualized communists as peasants with pitchforks who overran positions in mass attacks.

"Those guys know what they're doing," he said.

"But they don't know what they're gonna meet!" Mike laughed. Then he suddenly looked at Harry and said, "Why didn't you tell me you didn't have a carbine." And before Brubaker could stop him, he dashed across the rice field, grabbed Nestor Gamidge's carbine and stripped the dead man of ammunition. Two F4U's, seeing what Mike was doing, roared low and held the communists off while the Irishman dodged and ducked his way back to the ditch.

"Boy, now they'll know something hit 'em!" he cried as he jammed the weapon into Harry's hands.

Realization that Mike intended to battle it out here made Harry shiver and he asked, "You think there's any chance they'd allow us to surrender?"

"Those apes?" Mike asked.

The two Americans piled the last rocks before their faces and Harry asked, "Why do you hate them so much?"

"Simple. One Sunday morning in the cathedral I heard the cardinal explain it all," Mike said. A bullet zinged into the mud behind them and Mike grabbed Brubaker's arm. "You understand, sir, I came out here to save you. I don't want to die. There was a fightin' chance or I wouldn't have come. But now we're here, let's go down really swingin'."

He watched one of the communists creep forward for a better shot. "Don't fire too soon at these apes," he whispered. He kept his hand on Harry's arm for at least two minutes. Then, just as the enemy soldier got into position Mike blasted him right in the face. When Mike looked back he saw that Brubaker was busy with his hip knife, slashing away at his poopy suit.

"What are you doin'?" the Irishman exploded.

"Letting some air in."

"Have you gone nuts, sir?"

"Ever since I climbed into my first poopy suit I've been weighed down. I've been sweating and unable to breathe. Like a zombie. Today I want to feel like a human being." He stripped away large chunks of his burdensome gear and stood reasonably free. "I feel better already," he said.

Mike was sure the lieutenant had gone off his rocker but there wasn't anything he could do about it so he laughed and said, "I'm the same way. I couldn't fight these apes without my green hat."

"Why do you wear that?" Harry asked.

"I want people to know I'm around."

"That's what you told the captain. But what's the real dope?"

Mike stopped, looked frankly at Brubaker and said, "When I was a kid we lived . . ." He stopped abruptly and asked, "Tell me the truth, sir, wasn't that captain a pathetic ape?"

"The way he used windmill all the time."

"In about three minutes now," Mike said, pointing to the trees.

The communists moved slowly and with deliberate plan. Four of them came in from the south, three from the mountain quarter. "I'm gonna keep my eye on those four out there," Mike said.

Some minutes passed and there was a flurry of fire from the three soldiers in the mountain quarter but Forney yelled, "Forget them!" and he was right for the other four lunged forward and tried to overrun the ditch. Calmly Mike and Harry waited until the communists were close upon them. Then they started to fire rapidly. The communists fired back but Mike yelled, "They're crumblin'," and he chopped them down.

"That'll take care of the boys," he shouted. "Now bring on the men." But as he turned to congratulate Brubaker an unseen communist who had sneaked in from the sea quarter hurled two grenades into the ditch. One of them Mike managed to throw back but as he lifted the second it exploded and tore him apart. His body, motivated by the driving forces that had occupied his mind, stumbled forward toward the unseen enemy and pitched into the snow.

Now the sky was empty and the helicopter stood burned out in the rice field and in the ditch there was no one beside him. Harry Brubaker, a twenty-nine-year-old lawyer from Denver, Colorado, was alone in a spot he had never intended to defend in a war he had not understood. In his home town at that moment the University of Colorado was playing Denver in their traditional basketball game. The stands were crowded with more than 8,000 people and not one of them gave a damn about Korea. In San Francisco a group of men were finishing dinner and because the Korean war was a vulnerable topic, they laid plans to lambaste it from one end of the country to the other, but none of them really cared about the war or sought to comprehend it. And in New York thousands of Americans were crowding into the night clubs where the food was good and the wine expensive, but hardly anywhere in the city except in a few homes whose men were overseas was there even an echo of Korea.

But Harry Brubaker was in Korea, armed with two carbines. He was no longer afraid nor was he resentful. This was the war he had been handed by his nation and in the noonday sun he had only one thought: he was desperately in love with his wife and kids and he wanted to see them one more time.

The memory of his family was too much to bear and for an instant he pressed his right hand across his eyes and thought, "The girls will be in the garden now. . . ."

He did not complete the picture for the hidden communist who had tossed the grenades had remained close and now with one carefully planned shot sped a bullet directly through the right hand that covered the American's face. In that millionth of a second, while ten slim Banshees roared in from the sea to resume command of the sky, Harry Brubaker understood in some fragmentary way the purpose of his being in Korea. But the brief knowledge served no purpose, for the next instant he plunged face down into the ditch.

Through the long afternoon that followed, Admiral Tarrant haunted his telephone, waiting word of the miracle that would save his son. When Mike Forney left the scow with his helicopter, the admiral had said, "Well, Mike'll get him." Then the leader of the F4U's reported the copter burning.

Now, from the clandestine broadcaster near Wonsan came the facts: "Jet plane crash. Helicopter crash. Three Americans killed by communist troops."

Shaken, the lean, hard-bitten admiral left flag plot and walked gravely to his tiny room, for he knew that he must report these facts to Nancy Brubaker, in Yokosuka. But as he stared at the paper he asked, "How do you explain to a wife that her husband has died for his nation? How do you tell that to a woman with two children?" And he thought of his own wife, sitting somewhere in a dark room knitting a child's garment . . . but it was already more than seven feet long.

The job was too much for him. Later, maybe, he would know what to write. Then he thought of the Cag, who had led this ill-starred mission. He burned with fury and summoned the Cag to him, lashing at the bullet-headed commander as soon as he appeared.

"Why was Brubaker abandoned?"

Cag's eyes were red and tired from too much flying but he controlled his nerves and said, "We kept an air cap over him."

"If one helicopter crashed, why didn't you send another?"

"Sir, it's not my job to dispatch copters. You ask for volunteers. And there are never enough Mike Forneys."

"How was Brubaker hit in the first place?"

"He was working over the dumps."

The admiral pounced on this. "What was he doing at the dumps?"

Patiently Cag explained. "Before we took off we agreed. If we get the bridges, we expend our ammo on the dumps."

Icily, from the empty bitterness of his bosom, the old man asked, "Was that wise?"

Cag had taken enough. He'd stood this angry old tyrant long enough and there was no promotion in the navy that would make him take any more. "Admiral," he said grimly, "this was a good mission. We did everything just right. I put Brubaker in charge of the third division because I could trust him to fly low and bore in with his bombs. He did just that."

Cag, trembling with anger, rushed on, "Admiral, everybody in the air group knows that you selected Brubaker as your special charge. You do that on every command and we know why you do it. Some kid your own boy's age. So today I led your boy to death. But it was a good mission. We did everything just right. And it was your boy who helped destroy the bridges. Admiral, if my eyes are red it's for that kid. Because he was mine too. And I lost him."

The old man stood there, staring stonily at the shaking commander with the bullet head while Cag shot the works. "I don't care any longer what kind of fitness report you turn in on me because this was a good mission. It was a good mission." Without saluting he stormed from flag country, his fiery steps echoing as he stamped away.

For many hours the admiral remained alone. Then toward morning he heard the anti-submarine patrol go out and as the engines roared he asked, "Why is America lucky enough to have such men? They leave this tiny ship and fly against the enemy. Then they must seek the ship, lost somewhere on the sea. And when they find it, they have to land upon its pitching deck. Where did we get such men?"

He went out to watch the launching of the dawn strike. As streaks of light appeared in the east, pilots came on deck. Bundled like animals awakened from hibernation, they waddled purposefully to their jets. The last to climb aboard was Cag, stocky and round like a snowball. He checked each jet, then studied his own. Finally, as if there were nothing more he could do, he scrambled into his plane and waited. Majestically, the task force turned into the wind, the bull horn jangled and a voice in the gloom cried, "Launch jets."

Admiral Tarrant watched them go, two by two from the lashing catapult, planes of immortal beauty whipping into the air with flame and fury upon them. They did not waste fuel orbiting but screamed to the west, seeking new bridges in Korea.

JAMES A. MICHENER, one of the world's most popular writers, was the author of the Pulitzer Prize–winning *Tales of the South Pacific*, the best-selling novels *Hawaii, Texas, Chesapeake, The Covenant,* and *Alaska,* and the memoir *The World Is My Home.* Michener served on the advisory council to NASA and the International Broadcast Board, which oversees the Voice of America. Among dozens of awards and honors, he received America's highest civilian award, the Presidential Medal of Freedom, in 1977, and an award from the President's Committee on the Arts and Humanities in 1983 for his commitment to art in America. Michener died in 1997 at the age of ninety.

## ABOUT THE TYPE

This book was set in Times Roman, designed by Stanley Morison (1889–1967) specifically for *The Times* of London. The typeface was introduced in the newspaper in 1932. Times Roman had its greatest success in the United States as a book and commercial typeface, rather than one used in newspapers.